Eric Wilder

Bones of Skeleton Creek

Gondwana Press

Edmond, Oklahoma

Other Books by Eric Wilder

Ghost of a Chance
Murder Etouffee
Name of the Game
A Gathering of Diamonds
Over the Rainbow
Big Easy
Just East of Eden
Lily's Little Cajun Cookbook
Of Love and Magic
City of Spirits
Primal Creatures
Black Magic Woman
River Road
Blink of an Eye

First published in 2010 as
Morning Mist of Dawn

Gondwana Press
1802 Canyon Park Cir. Ste C
Edmond, OK 73013

For information on books by Eric Wilder
www.ericwilder.com

Front Cover by Andrés Grau
http://andresgrau.tumblr.com/

Gondwana Edition
First Printing – 2017

ISBN: 978-1-946576-02-6

Acknowledgments

Thanks to Terry Felts, former death investigator, and Gary Kinney, Oklahoma County Deputy Sheriff for their input involving police and investigative matters, and Andres Grau for his wonderfully evocative cover. I also wish to thank my wife Marilyn because she's always there for me with words of encouragement when I need them.

For Marilyn

Bones
of Skeleton Creek

A novel by
Eric Wilder

Chapter 1

Buck McDivit's old pickup backfired as he pulled into a parking space in front of the Second Bank of Edmond and turned off the engine. When he entered the heavy glass doors, a woman at the front desk asked him if he needed assistance.

"I have an appointment with Jeb Johnson. I'm a few minutes early," he said.

She smiled and nodded as he walked past her to the banker's office. Johnson's mousy secretary continued shuffling papers on her desk, glancing briefly over the top of her glasses at him.

"Mr. Johnson's on the phone. Have a seat, and I'll tell him you're here."

Twenty minutes later her intercom buzzed,

and she motioned Buck that the banker was ready to talk to him. The little man didn't bother standing, pointing instead to the lone chair in front of his desk. Though Buck had known Jeb Johnson most of his life, the banker didn't bother saying hello.

"Don't have much time, so tell me what you need," he said.

"My old beater has two hundred thousand miles on it," Buck said. "Maintenance is eating me up. I need a loan to buy a new truck."

"Your credit score is less than seven hundred. You got no steady job and not much in the way of assets. I can't risk the bank's money on this one. We're going to have to pass," Johnson said.

Buck felt as if someone had kicked him in the groin as he stared at the little man with a voice much deeper than his size indicated.

"I've never had a loan go south. You know that, Jeb."

"Things change," Johnson said, peering over his reading glasses. "The auditors would have my ass in a sling if I made this loan. Unless of course if you put twenty percent down."

"I don't have that kind of money."

"Then maybe you don't need a new forty thousand dollar pickup. You know what the monthly payments are on a loan that big? Hell, Buck, what's the matter with the truck you got?"

"Like I said, Jeb, it's on its last leg."

"Then lower your standards because you can't afford a new truck." The little man whisked his hand through his thinning hair before glancing at his watch. "Now, I got another appointment coming in after lunch, so I'm leaving a little early. Anything else I can help you with?"

Buck didn't bother answering because Jeb Johnson had already grabbed his overcoat and headed out of the office. Pulling the collar of his jean jacket up around his neck, he followed him through the front door to Broadway, Edmond's main street.

Buck's boots were old though always polished and well maintained. He had long legs, and his jeans and Western shirt made him seem taller than he really was. Two women passing on the sidewalk turned to give the handsome young cowboy with expressive brown eyes and dark wavy hair a second glance. Still upset about his meeting with the banker, he didn't notice.

Edmond, a former train stop had grown into a north suburb of sprawling Oklahoma City. No longer a bedroom community for the wealthy, it was now the home of the third largest university in the state, and the third-biggest city in Oklahoma.

Traffic in the thriving little metropolis was nowhere close to the giant jam that was Dallas though it was heading in that direction. It also had a hundred fifty churches and at least ten Starbucks. Cold gusty wind whistled down the street, chilling the back of his neck, as someone tapped his shoulder.

"Sorry to bother you, mister. I ain't ate in two days. Can you spare a dollar?"

The economy, as in other parts of the country, had begun collapsing in Oklahoma. Now it seemed panhandlers populated every major cross street in the city. This was the first one Buck had seen in downtown Edmond. The man was scruffy, his clothes dirty and torn. The dog he held with a short strand of rope around its neck caught his attention.

The young black and white border collie wagged its tail and licked Buck's hand when he reached down to pet it. Fishing out his wallet, he glanced at his last twenty.

"What's your dog's name?" he asked.

"Ain't got no name."

Buck handed him the twenty. "I don't have anything smaller. Guess it's your lucky day." He pulled the bill back when the man reached for it. "You have to promise me part of this will go to feed your dog."

The little man snatched the bill from Buck's hand and stuffed it into his shirt pocket.

"He ain't my dog. I was gonna tie the little pest to a park bench and be rid of it. If you want him, you better take him cause he ain't staying with me."

Buck thought for a moment about punching the ratty little man in the nose and taking back his twenty. Instead, he took the rope and watched as he hurried away, probably to the nearest liquor store.

When Buck squatted to rub the little dog's ears, the beautiful animal rewarded him with a friendly bark. Wagging his tail, he licked Buck's hand.

"Maybe I can put an ad in the paper and find a good home for you."

Feeling suddenly depressed because of his loan rejection, he wondered if he should move north to Logan County and the less pretentious town of Guthrie. Someone he recognized exited the coffee shop across the street, interrupting his malaise. Waving, he crossed the narrow street, the dog wagging his tail as he followed him.

Unlike sprawling Oklahoma City, no skyscrapers jutted into the clouds in downtown Edmond. Few structures exceeded more than two stories, and those were mostly brick and native rock buildings. The people walking along the sidewalks moved at the slow pace of what was once a small town.

Clayton O'Meara, his ex-employer, had apparently not seen him and was heading in the opposite direction. He stopped when Buck called his name.

"Trying to avoid me, Clayton?"

The man grinned, showing a set of teeth a little too perfect for someone his age. He stood several inches taller than Buck, probably six foot four, and he sported a full head of silver hair, complete with expensive salon highlights.

"Hey, Buck. Nice leash you got. What are you doing up so early?"

"I was about to ask you the same thing?" he said, ignoring Clayton's comment about the dog's makeshift leash.

Clayton answered Buck's question with little more than a wry grin.

"Business. Don't you ever feed that dog?"

"He's not really mine."

"From the way he's wagging his tail I'd say he thinks he is."

A wealthy oilman, Clayton O'Meara owned a cattle spread in Logan County. He rarely left his showplace ranch, and Buck couldn't recall ever seeing him in downtown Edmond. Despite the chilling temperature, the older man wore no hat, probably so as not to distract from his full head of hair. Only an unzipped orange goose down parka emblazoned with the letters OSU covered his designer sports shirt.

Clayton was at least thirty years older than Buck. Didn't matter because the sparkle in his hazy eyes made him seem little more than a teenager. Glancing at his Rolex Commander, as if the expensive watch somehow held the answer to some unasked question, he pointed to his car down the street.

"I'm sort of in a hurry."

Buck recognized the brush-off.

"Didn't mean to hold you up," he said.

Clayton grinned and slapped Buck's shoulder. "Sorry to rush. Got an appointment, and I gotta get.

We can catch up on things later."

Instead of hurrying away, he turned toward the door of the coffee shop he'd just exited. Reaching for the handle as if he had forgotten something inside, he thought better of it. Pivoting on the heels of his polished snakeskin boots, he headed down the street to his waiting vehicle. Buck watched as Clayton's chauffeur opened the back door of a big white Mercedes for him. With tires squealing, the car disappeared around the corner.

Buck glanced at the door of Café Oklahoma, the coffee shop a fixture in downtown Edmond for almost as long as he could remember. He knew Clayton well enough to know he wasn't a coffee drinker. Curious, he opened the door and glanced inside.

Seeing a familiar face alone at a table, he forgot about Clayton as memories of a recent romance, ended too soon for his liking flooded his psyche. It was his former girlfriend, Kay Karson. Everyone called her KK. She turned around as if expecting someone else. Seeing him, she folded her arms, frowned, and glanced away.

"No greeting for an old friend?" Buck said.

KK crossed her shapely legs. Considering the length of the short leather skirt she was wearing, black lace hose and ankle-length boots were her only concessions to the outside chill.

"You're really full of yourself, aren't you?"

Before he could answer, an employee said, "Sir, you can't bring your dog in here."

"I'll only be a minute," he said.

Buck and KK had been an item for almost a year. She liked line dancing, prancing horses, and ice-cold Coors beer. Her slender legs looked great in tight blue jeans and cowboy boots. Honey blond hair draped her shoulders, framing her slightly less than perfect though unforgettable face.

She was, in fact, a beauty queen, having amassed three titles before the tender age of eighteen. Buck soon learned she thoroughly realized the effect she had on men. Now, at twenty-nine, she could focus her power on the opposite sex like an ICBM, with much the same explosive result. Buck had found his dream woman. At least he'd thought.

KK's father was a medical doctor in Tulsa, her mother a college professor at Tulsa University. She had never wanted for anything. Looking at her now, Buck could see she had acquired a few very expensive trinkets he doubted even her doting dad could afford.

A diamond pendant graced her slender neck. The large diamond in an expensive setting had good color and was no fake. It was a companion piece to the diamond ring on her finger that sported an even larger and more ostentatious stone. Mink lined her gloves and the expensive jacket draped across the back of the booth.

"Just saying hi to an old friend," he said.

KK tipped over a half-empty coffee cup with her elbow. Dabbing at the spot with a napkin, she continued to frown.

"You call yourself an investigator. You don't have a clue. I imagine you must have thought all you had to do was smile at me and I would jump back into your bed like a horny teenager. Well, we're not in college, and you are not the star quarterback and campus heartthrob anymore. You don't even have a real job. Your nice ass doesn't compliment your lousy future."

She didn't wait for his reply, brushing past him and appearing not to hear his comeback.

"Guess tamales and dancing Saturday night are out of the question."

As she disappeared out the door without looking back, he wondered what he could have done to provoke such a display of anger. With a shrug to the employee, he followed her outside, watching as she climbed into a white Mercedes sports car, and gunned away down the street.

"No problem," he said to himself. "I can't afford a date Saturday night anyway."

Two rejections and a brush-off before noon, he thought as he considered where she had acquired the Mercedes and her expensive mink jacket. Their relationship had not ended badly. It had simply flickered and died.

Buck had attended college for a while. He'd dropped out to sign on with the O.C.P.D. One of his friends on the force had left to become an oil and gas lease broker during one of the many oil booms, and Buck soon followed. His lucrative job ended during an unexpected, at least to him, reduction in oil prices.

Since then, he had supported himself in many different jobs such as club bouncer, skip tracer, process server, and private detective. His opportunities for gainful employment had recently narrowed, and he found himself using his meager savings to pay his bills. It didn't help that his aging Dodge pickup needed repair almost weekly.

"Come on, buddy. Let's get you something to eat."

When Buck reached his truck and unlocked the door, his cheeks burned hot. He'd never had an ego problem, even though gorgeous women often grew speechless upon meeting him. It didn't matter because now he needed a drink, preferably something with whiskey in it. Shaking his head, he remembered he couldn't afford one. Past lunchtime, his stomach growled. After stopping at a convenience store, he searched for change in the truck's console.

"Wait here. I'll be right back."

He returned a few minutes later with a hot dog.

Giving the meat to the dog, he ate the bun and chili. The little border collie gobbled down the wiener then curled up and went to sleep in the passenger seat.

Buck had not reached the horse ranch where he lived and worked part time when he received a call from the Logan County death investigator. One of his many jobs included assisting the investigator whenever a suspicious death occurred. He did not care for the often-gory work. It didn't matter now. Because of his current financial situation, he could ill afford to turn down a job, no matter how distasteful.

A cowboy had discovered a body at a nearby ranch. Clayton O'Meara's ranch. Buck pondered the coincidence as he turned his truck around and headed north, along with his sleepy passenger.

Chapter 2

Muted sunlight peeked through a thick cover of clouds as Buck stood in a semicircle with a group of men, waiting for the arrival of the death investigator. Not knowing what to expect, he let the young dog out of the truck. He was curious but kept his distance from the men. After checking the perimeter around the truck, he wallowed a spot and stretched out to observe the scene.

No one spoke as a gray van backed up to the location. Already probably a banner day for homicides in Logan County, the person exiting the van was Satchel Pratt instead of Doc Watson, the usual man for the job. A chill wind whipped tree limbs at the nearby ranch house. It didn't matter to Satchel Pratt, his only protection from the weather a light jacket imprinted with the words death investigator. Satchel's horn rims did little to impart an air of studiousness to the large man with dark hair pulled back in a ponytail.

"Nice dog, Cowboy. What's up?" he asked Buck, ignoring the other half-dozen law officers and ranch hands standing around, waiting for something to happen.

"Dead cowpoke needing your expertise."

Understanding fully someone was bullshitting

him, Pratt smiled and tapped Buck's shoulder.

"I'll do my best," he said.

Clayton's large ranch was several miles west of the I-35 corridor, the mournful horn of a distant semi barely discernible. Buck could see the house, barns, and many outbuildings through a mist rising up from the pasture. A grove of stunted trees north of the fencerow marked the course of Skeleton Creek, the deeply incised streambed filled with water only during rainy parts of the year.

The interstate highway came out of Dallas, heading north through Oklahoma City and Wichita. Local law enforcement usually had a field day along the route, intersecting tons of illegal drugs coming from Mexico. Crows flying overhead voiced their displeasure with the disturbance going on below. Buck also noticed Clayton's cows, herding up in anticipation of their dinner. They seemed to sense something horrible had happened, and he wondered if the dead man was the person that usually fed them.

No one had approached the body, wary of destroying evidence at what was obviously a gruesome crime scene. It was the body of a male, his legs bent at the knees and folded beneath him in what would have been a most uncomfortable position. If he were alive to notice. He wasn't.

A crumpled felt Stetson covered the man's face and one of the deputies took a step back when Satchel removed the hat. Opened wide, the dead man's eyes stared back at them. Buck guessed the person's age at late-twenties, early-thirties, his dark hair yet to show any gray. He had the muscular frame of a weight lifter and seemed in good physical condition. Other than, what had caused his demise.

The first job of a death investigator is to check for trauma, something causing the inopportune demise. Sometimes trauma is not apparent. No such problem existed with this death. The man was quite naked and lying in a puddle of blood pooled mostly beneath his buttocks. Satchel Pratt pulled on a pair of rubber gloves and knelt beside the victim. From his black bag, he removed a syringe he used to extract a sample of blood from the victim's femoral artery.

Pratt had a sheath on his belt from which he took what looked like a meat thermometer. After labeling the blood sample, he deftly inserted it beneath the right side of the man's rib cage, directing the instrument into the dead man's liver. The lead cop, a Logan County Sheriff's deputy, stepped closer. Satchel wiped off the thermometer with a cloth and placed it back in the sheath.

"Can I borrow your pen?" he asked the deputy.

The dead man's head rested in a mess of blood, bone, and brains. Gently lifting it, Satchel inserted the pen into the gaping hole.

"This is the exit wound," he said.

The man's bloodless lips formed a grotesque smile, a dribble of blood on both sides of the mouth. The second stage of rigor had set in, and Satchel had to open his jaws with a plastic Archimedes screw. He used the opening to probe inside with the Deputy's pen. After removing it, he offered it back to the man.

"You keep it," the deputy said, shaking his head and taking a step backward.

Satchel grinned, one Buck had seen many times. It was all part of his shtick, and he performed it for the benefit of dupes that hadn't yet observed the scene of a homicide, and for the entertainment of others that had. Zipping down his light jacket, he slid the pen into his shirt pocket. His performance not yet complete, he anticipated the Deputy's next question.

"How long has he been dead?"

Buck tried hard to keep from smiling as

Satchel removed a second meat thermometer he kept sheathed on the right side of his belt. Holding it close to his myopic eyes, he touched the instrument to his tongue. Both deputies and the three cowboys, not realizing the instrument was not the one Satchel had inserted into the man's liver, gasped.

"Maybe as long as twelve hours," Satchel said, "But it could be less. It's fairly cold, and I can't say with certainty."

Seeing the men's stunned reaction, Buck could contain himself no longer, breaking into an uncontrolled bout of boisterous laughter. It stopped abruptly when a familiar voice spoke behind him.

"What's so funny, McDivit?"

Buck knew without turning it was Logan County, Sheriff Jim Hagen.

Buck didn't bother answering because he knew the sheriff had witnessed Satchel's little act on more than one occasion. Someone much taller than Sheriff Hagen and someone he'd already seen once that day, accompanied him—Clayton O'Meara, owner of the ranch on which the dead man was murdered. Clayton smiled at Buck and nodded.

"What's the story here, Satchel?" Hagen asked.

"Well, Sheriff, I'd say you got yourself another homicide."

Buck took notes as Satchel Pratt began to recite.

"Caucasian male, in great physical condition, and no older than thirty-five. Someone brought him into this clearing about ten to twelve hours ago and forced him to strip off his clothes. They tied his hands behind his back with chicken wire and had him kneel. Then they castrated him. While he was still alive considering the amount of blood on the ground. They stuck a weapon in his mouth and pulled the trigger."

"Sounds more like suicide to me," the sheriff said. "No one would let a shooter stick a pistol in their mouth."

The deputy snickered, but turned his head away when Pratt said, "You mean you would start resisting right after you cut your own balls off?"

Sheriff Hagen shook his head. "I'm just saying when somebody dies from a gunshot wound in the mouth, it's usually suicide. What's your take on it, Buck?"

"Whoever sliced him up took more than his balls. From the cuts on his chest, it almost looks like someone was trying to skin him alive. Maybe the murderer gave him the option to kill himself."

"Satchel, sound about right?"

"I'd say at least part of Mr. McDivit's story holds water, except that the victim's hands were bound behind his back. I don't know how he could have pulled off that little trick. Then again I'm not a professional fiction writer."

It was Buck's turn to smile. Perhaps he had concocted too much of a story. Didn't really matter because he wasn't the lead homicide detective, only an assistant to the death investigator who had voiced his opinion when asked.

Sheriff Hagen seemed to agree with Buck's theory. "What else?"

Everyone, including Satchel Pratt, turned their attention to Buck when he said, "There were three men on horseback here last night."

"How do you know?" Hagen asked.

"It's getting dark, and I'm not as good a tracker as my Cherokee godfather, but the ground is damp, and a blind man can see the tracks."

Glancing at the big man standing beside him, Sheriff Hagen asked, "Your men?"

Clayton shook his head. "Don't have a clue.

We can ask my foreman.”

“You recognize the victim?”

“Frank Boggs, one of my best hands. Been with me since I bought this ranch. Had an apartment on the place and lived here full time. My foreman can get you all the information we have on him.”

“What else?” Hagen asked.

“Good looking man with an eye for the ladies. Had more girlfriends than a stray tomcat.”

“Think maybe this is a revenge killing, maybe by a jilted lover? What do you think, Satchel?” he asked.

“Don’t think so, sheriff,” Satchel said.

“Why not?”

“Whoever killed your cowboy here was someone more physically imposing than the victim. In my opinion, the killer was a large, powerful male.”

Sheriff Hagen glanced at his lead deputy, still ashen-faced from observing Satchel’s little performance joke.

“Get your head out of it, Lamont. Tape off the crime scene, get pictures and start combing the area for evidence. Don’t look like we’ll find much, though you never know.”

Clayton turned to leave, shaking his head, and motioning his gawking cowpokes to accompany him. He glanced at Buck before leaving.

The dog had remained by the truck, keeping a vigilant eye on the proceedings. He was smart, and it had taken him no time at all to learn his boundaries, a quality Buck instantly noticed and appreciated. Satchel also noticed.

“One fine dog you got there. How much did you pay for him?”

“Twenty bucks,” Buck said with a grin.

“I’ll give you fifty.”

"Sorry. I'm starting to get attached."

"Yeah, what's his name?"

"He doesn't have one yet."

"I'd call him Pard if he were mine." When the dog's ears perked up, Satchel said, "See, he even recognizes it."

The day had started out cold and had only grown colder. Satchel was a seasoned death investigator and had already determined much more from the body than he'd told Sheriff Hagen. It seemed unlikely Buck would ever see the investigation through to fruition, so he didn't linger on the thought for long.

As he and Satchel finished their work, the murder scene began to look like a washed-out oil painting. The end of a long day, wet flakes of snow began falling from an ashen sky as they rolled the dead man in a gurney to the back of Satchel's van.

Chapter 3

Buck's morning started unexpectedly with a wet tongue licking his face.

"Morning, Pard. I bet you need to go outside."

After a glance at his old Rolex, he crawled out of bed. It was still two hours before daylight. Buck lived on a thoroughbred horse farm in eastern Oklahoma County. The wealthy woman that owned the place provided him with an apartment on the second floor of the million-dollar barn in exchange for certain daily tasks, mostly feeding and exercising the horses on the farm. Not an easy job because the big animals from time to time numbered almost fifty.

Buck didn't mind because it gave him a roof over his head. He also loved the horses, and they loved him. He knew every animal by name, and if they liked carrots or apples. He went outside with Pard. When he finally stumbled back upstairs to the bathroom, he dabbed his face with cold water from the tap.

Pouring a can of beef stew from the pantry into a bowl, he sat it on the floor by a water bowl. The dog's tail never stopped wagging as he cleaned the bowl.

Upon stepping into the shower, a warm stream of water soon dispersed his dreams and returned him to reality. By the time he had toweled the drops off his broad shoulders, he felt good as new again, or at least better than he had when he awoke.

Mrs. O'Meara's former boyfriend, a horse trainer less than half her age, had taken a new job in Kentucky. Jilted, she lost interest in her farm and began traveling extensively. Now, she was in Scotland. Buck adored everything about the thoroughbred farm but hated fending off her constant advances. Not that she was hideous or even unattractive. Hell, she looked and acted a lot like Ann-Margret. Her recent absence from the place still came as a relief.

Virginia O'Meara had acquired the farm in a divorce settlement from her former husband, Clayton. Clayton didn't mind. His passions were oil, cattle, and women, and not necessarily in that order. He had only bought the farm to satisfy Virginia's whim. She was rich enough in her own right to afford it without him. The daughter of old Oklahoma wealth, she liked the trappings money brought her and cared little that Clayton's fondness for her had lots to do with a pending merger with her granddad's old-line oil company.

Buck's apartment was more than he needed with its mahogany paneling, expensive carpeting, and real gold faucets in the bathroom. It also had a relaxing balcony overlooking the training track that afforded a scenic view of much of the farm. He was glancing out the window at a trainer, working a horse on the track, when the phone rang.

"That you, Buck?"

He instantly recognized Clayton O'Meara's whiskey-wracked voice. After divorcing Virginia, the rich oilman had bought a ranch in nearby Logan County, his house more like a ski lodge than ranch house, its tall ceilings beamed with freshly hewn timbers. American Indian art and mounted animal trophies occupied every wall, bearskin rugs the polished wood floors. Buck loved to visit, sitting on the veranda at night, sipping whiskey and listening to coyotes howl.

"What's up, Clayton?"

"Seeing you twice yesterday got me thinking. You're just the man I need to help me. Drop by the ranch, and we'll talk about it."

After buying dog food from a nearby convenience store, Buck drove to Clayton O'Meara's ranch. Pard had taken the passenger seat as his own and stood in the open window, his tail wagging. They found the ornate electronic gate already open, signaling Clayton was expecting him. There were guards lurking somewhere near.

Usually when he visited they would hassle him unmercifully, making him wait a half hour or more before allowing him to continue down the winding road to Clayton's ranch house. Today, no one bothered him.

O'Meara employed at least thirty hands on the large spread, many of them solely for security reasons. Clayton was big on security, and it had surprised Buck to see him alone in downtown Edmond without a single bodyguard. The thought crossed his mind as he passed through the gate.

They followed the narrow blacktop road through landscaped acres of manicured lawn toward Clayton's house. Cottonwood trees along the creek were leafless, awaiting spring. When Buck exited his truck, he glimpsed an armed cowboy watching him from the open loft of a distant barn.

Leaving the window open, Buck said, "Wait for me Pard. I won't be long."

Buck had visited Woolaroc, vacation retreat of oilman Frank Phillips, and Clayton's rough-hewn log house reminded him of it. If anything, it was even larger and more eclectic. He entered the back entrance of the enclosed veranda without knocking. Sipping a glass of straight Kentucky bourbon, Clayton greeted him.

"Too early for me," Buck said, waving away Clayton's offer of whiskey. "Coffee, maybe."

Clayton snapped his fingers at someone behind the door.

"Seems this young man is too righteous to drink morning whiskey, Maria. Bring him some coffee instead."

Clayton's house was massive, its out-of-place southern-style veranda his favorite spot. Buck could see why as he settled into a comfortable rattan rocking chair located next to the older man's leather recliner. Clayton liked anything expensive, and the veranda's teak floor emulated the deck of a sultan's yacht.

An antique brass telescope and wheelhouse from a luxury riverboat sustained the nautical motif. The veranda wrapped around part of the house, including Clayton's bedroom. Its sliding glass door was ajar, a pair of eyes peeking through the bedroom curtain. Clayton had obviously just come from there, his bathrobe covering his pajamas.

Clayton had grown up in a lower middle-class Edmond family and had attended OSU on a football scholarship. His PE degree had gotten him a sales job with an international cementing company's Oklahoma branch. He eventually started his own oil company utilizing the many contacts he'd made as a salesperson.

Clayton's primary talent was raising investor money. Raise it he did, parlaying it into a dynasty while never letting on his PE degree was in physical education and not petroleum engineering.

Though Buck had known Clayton for years,

most of the dirt on him had come from Clayton's ex-wife, Virginia, usually when she was in her cups and putting the moves on him. Being an information junkie, he listened to her stories, even if it sometimes got him into trouble. He'd been able to avoid a messy situation with the amorous-minded older woman, at least so far.

Clayton's housekeeper and general assistant around the house appeared with a cup of strong black coffee for Buck.

"Thanks, Maria. You always remember just the way I like it."

Middle-aged and slightly dumpy, she smiled without replying to the compliment. When Clayton sipped his whiskey and moved to the porch swing, Buck joined him following a sneezing fit.

"Allergies?"

Buck nodded. "This time every year. At least your cottonwoods aren't blooming. When are you going to cut them down?"

"Never," Clayton answered. You'd complain about a sharp stick in the eye."

"You know me too well," Buck said with a grin. "Maybe we should discuss your problem now."

Clayton slammed the whiskey in one gulp. "This might take a while because I have more than one."

His frown and furrowed brow indicated something was distressing him. His ranch was large by Oklahoma standards, and it included llamas, peacocks, and other exotic animals. He also ran a large herd of cattle. Buck sipped his coffee, waiting for Clayton to tell him what was bothering him.

"I lost a cow the other night. Sheriff Hagen thinks coyotes or bobcats are the likely culprits. He even suggested for me not to worry about it."

"Why would he say that?"

"Because I got bigger fish to fry."

"Last night's murder on your property?"

Clayton scratched his chin. "The murder is another matter. Hell, it might even be connected. Something got one of my cows, and whatever did it wasn't a coyote or a bobcat. You got time to take a look?"

"Nothing on my dance card today."

Clayton grinned and excused himself for a minute, disappearing through the curtains into his bedroom. He returned fully dressed, donning his cowboy hat and wool-lined leather coat Maria had brought him, as if on cue. After a glance at the dancing curtain in Clayton's bedroom to see if someone was still peeking at them, Buck followed him out the back door where a tan Jeep awaited, its key already in the ignition.

"Mind if I bring my dog?"

Clayton flashed one of his patented smiles. "You said yesterday it wasn't your dog."

"Things change."

When Buck whistled, Pard bounded out of the truck's open window and joined them, jumping into the Jeep's backseat.

"Smart dog," Clayton said.

Chapter 4

The old Jeep had no top or windshield. Clayton cranked the engine and pulled forward almost before Buck had a chance to crawl in. There were no seatbelts.

"Most of my herd winters in the pastures just north of here. There are plenty of trees and gullies to break the north wind and two large ponds for water," Clayton said, driving with one hand and rubbing Pard's head with the other.

They followed a bumpy dirt road bordered for some distance by large rolls of hay. Buck could see part of the herd in the distance, mostly stout-shouldered Black Angus with a few Texas Longhorns mixed in for conversation sake. There were even a few deer munching on a bale of hay. A clump of blackjack trees appeared in the distance and Clayton headed toward them. Pard didn't bark or miss a thing.

They stopped along the way to go through two gates, Buck stepping out of the Jeep to open them. Blackjacks bounded Skeleton Creek that had incised the mostly flat ranchland, sometimes to a depth of nearly a hundred feet. The old Jeep screeched to a halt near the edge of the trees.

Clayton stepped out of the old vehicle. "We'll have to walk from here."

Buck and Pard followed the large man down the steep slope, neither out of breath when they reached the creek bed, full of water from the recent snowfall. Thick tree growth and shadows obliterated a dull sky. They soon came to a path leading up the slope to the other side.

"Deer path," Clayton explained after sloshing across the creek and starting up the slope. "Along with every other creature you can imagine."

They dragged themselves up the final few feet of the ravine with the help of a hanging vine. Buck and Pard followed him to a clearing where they saw and smelled the carcass of a cow. Pard circled it, not getting too close.

"One of yours?" Buck asked.

"It's mine all right."

Buck walked around the dead cow, studying the cuts and slashes on its black hide.

"The sheriff was right. Something did a job on this one."

"One big and powerful animal."

"Like what?"

Clayton paused only briefly before answering, "I think it's a panther."

Buck had heard tales all his life from farmers and ranchers in the area about their panther sightings. Most were only slightly more credible than having seen a UFO. Still, belief in the presence of big cats in central Oklahoma persisted, and the wounds on the carcass of Clayton's cow did nothing to belie the legend.

"You didn't bring me here just to see a dead cow. What else is on your mind?"

Clayton's smile turned into a frown. "I didn't want to talk about it back at the ranch."

"I'm listening."

"I started noticing about a month ago that I'm

missing some cows."

"Very many cows?"

"No, just a few."

"With the size of your herd, how in the world would you know if you'd lost one or two?"

Clayton nudged a red sandstone rock with the toe of his boot, and then glanced up at the morning's gray sky.

"Every animal has a numbered ear tag. We use the tags, so we'll know if they get their shots, keep tabs on how old they are and so on. The information's in a computer database, and there's not much I don't know about my herd. I think you can help me find out what's going on."

"You have thirty hands on this spread. You don't need me."

Clayton pointed to a slow-moving pumping unit in the nearby clearing. "See that oil well over there? One of those storage tanks holds about two hundred barrels, about fifteen grand worth of oil at seventy-five dollars a barrel. All a thief has to do is drive on the lease at three in the morning, back a bobtail up to the spigot, fill it and drive away. Oil is virtually untraceable. You can't tell one barrel from the next. It's a perfect crime."

"What's your point?"

"My point is there's never an oil theft without a company man knowing about it. The pumper gauges every tank, every day and knows how much oil is in each one of them. Oil thieves don't drive up to a random oil well and chance being caught robbing a tank with only a few barrels in it. They usually work with the company pumper who tells them which well to hit. The oil thief has a nice payday, and the company man gets a cut."

"You think one of your hands is involved in the theft of your cattle?"

"Not just my cattle. I think someone is systematically stealing crude from Crescent Oil."

"Any ideas?"

"Someone that knows about my cattle and oil business."

"Can't be very many people."

"Nope, just one. Roy Dunlap, the President of Crescent Oil."

"Roy is your close friend, or am I mistaken?"

"Best friend."

"You think your best friend is stealing from you?"

"That's where you come in. Consider yourself on my personal payroll starting today."

"Won't Roy be suspicious?"

"He and everyone else need to stay in the dark. I already told him you are a consultant doing due diligence for someone considering buying part of my oil and cattle holdings. You'll have access to company records, and he won't know what you're really looking for."

"I'll need to get a look at your cattle database, and the employment records of all your hands."

"Consider it done. Roy is expecting you. He has an office ready and will supply you with a computer with all the information you need, including my ranch records."

Clayton grinned when Buck asked, "What else is on your mind?"

"Since you're on the payroll, you may as well help me with all my problems. You got time to listen?"

"I have all day."

"I started buying land around this ranch years ago. I managed to put together four sections. Almost." Clayton pointed toward the Cimarron River Buck knew lay just beyond a distant grove of blackjacks. "There are two hundred acres right smack in the middle of my ranch I don't own. I've offered ten thousand an acre for the property. Can't get them to sell."

"Who can afford to turn down that kind of money?"

Clayton frowned to show his disgust. "A commune populated by a crazy bunch of women."

"If they won't take ten thousand dollars an acre, what can I do about it?"

"You got ways with women. Nose around and see if you can influence things for me. Even if they don't sell, I'd still like to know as much about the place as possible. Talk with the people in charge. Find out what they are up too. While you're at it, I'd like you to keep up with Frankie Boggs' murder. I don't expect you to solve it, but see what you can turn up."

"You give me more credit than I deserve when it comes to women. I'll look into the compound for you, and the murder. While we're here, though, let's look around."

"Good, you impressed me last night with your tracking skills. I didn't know you were an Indian."

"Isn't everyone in Oklahoma?"

"Guess you're right about that," Clayton said.

Buck's Cherokee godfather had made sure he had developed a knack for tracking. The key was to look for something out of place, a footprint, a broken twig. He walked in an expanding circle around the dead cow, searching for anything anomalous. Despite the animal's wounds, he saw no sign of a struggle, not even a drop of blood on the ground.

After nearly ten minutes of silence, Clayton could no longer contain his curiosity. "What do you think?"

Buck shook his head. "Whatever killed your steer must be a ghost."

"You're kidding?"

Buck glanced up from the ground and slowly scanned the surroundings. Seeing nothing out of the ordinary, he followed Pard, sniffing at a nearby clump of bushes. Sinuous vines, lined with sharp barbs, formed an almost impenetrable mass of undergrowth. Buck grabbed a bush, revealing a path when he pulled it aside.

"Good boy, Pard."

They navigated the narrow path with care, occasionally stopping to extract briars from their jeans, and soon reached the edge of the ravine. The narrow path led down to the creek. Grasping vines and vegetation, Buck followed Pard down the steep path. When he reached the bottom, he grabbed Clayton, sliding perilously toward him.

"You okay?"

"If we ever get out of here."

Already busy studying the creek bed, Buck didn't comment. Erosion had diverted the main course. What remained was a gravel-lined draw that took a different direction than the creek. The draw, surrounded by underbrush and the ravine's steep walls formed a nearly invisible pathway. Buck, with Clayton in tow, followed Pard until the path widened.

A pristine pool of water lay near the center of the dry channel Africans would call a wadi. Buck knelt down to get a better view of something Pard was nosing near the clay edge of the pool.

"What is it?" Clayton asked.

"Pugmark," Buck said, moving aside to give Clayton a glimpse. He pointed at the impression of an animal's footprint in the clay. "I'd say whatever made it was one big cat."

Clayton studied the pugmark, and then asked, "What's your dog got in his mouth?"

Buck took the object from Pard. "One of those LED headlamps hunters use when they're illegally spotting game at night."

<hr>

Clayton barely stopped talking during the short drive back to the ranch. Buck only nodded when he said, "I told you I had a panther on my place. Now maybe someone will believe me. That was a panther track; wasn't it, Buck?"

"Yes sir, it was."

"Then where the hell did it come from?"

"Since big cats are free roaming it's impossible to say. Probably just kept moving until he found a place that suited him."

"But why here?"

"You have a big spread with lots of trees, rocks, and shelter, plenty of water and wild game and almost no humans around. You are a mile from a major highway and most of the section-line roads dead end when they reach your property. What more could any wild animal ask for?"

"Why hasn't someone seen him before now?"

"You saw the trail where we found the track. We were probably the first humans to lay eyes on that little pool of water, except the person who lost the headlamp. The cat has a lair somewhere near and sleeps during the day and hunts at night, mostly for wild turkeys, rabbits, and feral pigs, I'd say."

"Should I send the boys out to hunt it down?"

"He has plenty to eat without attacking your herd. Your cow was somewhere it wasn't supposed to be. I suspect it would be alive today if he hadn't been where we found it. My question to you is how did she get all the way across Skeleton Creek?"

Clayton had no answer. "I'll have the boys run the fence line and see if they can find a break."

"Have them do a head count while they're at it," Buck said. "Probably has something to do with the horse tracks we saw near the murder scene."

"Won't it tip them off I'm suspicious?"

"Just because you think someone is rustling your cows doesn't mean you believe one of your hands is responsible. Do a headcount. When you find that some are missing, and we both know you will report it to Sheriff Hagen. If nothing else, it may slow the rustlers down until we can get a handle on things. We might even flush a nervous quail or two."

When they reached the ranch, Clayton pulled the Jeep next to Buck's truck and handed him an envelope.

"Your first month's wages, an unlimited credit card and keys to your company car. You'll find it in the parking garage at the Petro Place."

Buck didn't argue. Clayton had already wheeled the Jeep around and headed for the barn. The sputtering engine of Buck's truck returned him to reality, as did the sight of the expensive white sports car parked next to Clayton's larger white Mercedes. It looked like the same car he had seen KK driving the previous day.

As he exited the open gate of Clayton's property, he pondered the implication. Pard, already taking a nap in the passenger seat, didn't share his concern.

Chapter 5

Hector Ramirez, Mrs. O'Meara's only full-time employee, agreed to keep an eye on Pard. Crescent Oil occupied two floors of the Petro Place Building, and Buck wasted no time getting there.

Roy Dunlap met Buck at the front door and hustled him down a long hallway, even before he'd had a chance to flirt with the pretty receptionist. Ushering him through the door of his large office, he shut it behind them.

Dunlap was probably in his sixties. Even with his snowy white hair, he seemed much younger. He had youthful green eyes and kept himself thin and fit, probably playing golf, and tennis. Only a loose layer of skin around his neck, covered mostly by his shirt collar and expensive tie, belied his true age.

"Grab a chair," he said, sitting behind an executive desk that must have cost Crescent Oil thousands of dollars.

He was immediately on the phone, ordering coffee from his secretary. Buck had barely settled into a leather chair when a very pretty woman entered without bothering to knock.

"Thanks so much, Georgia," Dunlap said, not

introducing the woman to Buck.

He glanced at her as she walked out the door. More than pretty, she was stunning with stylishly short, honey-blonde hair and big eyes a soft shade of blue that seemed almost too perfect to be real. Buck noticed her short skirt and athletic legs as she exited the office. From her grin, it was apparent she noticed him noticing.

Roy Dunlap also noticed. Tapping his desk to get Buck's attention, he offered him a cup of coffee from Georgia's carafe. After a sip, Dunlap's icy stare disappeared. Inhaling deeply, he leaned back in his expensive executive chair.

"You know Clayton as well as me. I don't know anyone more interested in security than him. The company records are for no one's eyes but yours, and what you are doing no one else's business except mine and Clay's."

Roy Dunlap finished his coffee and motioned Buck to follow, leading him down the long hallway to an office near the water cooler. Though much smaller than the one they had just vacated, the office seemed fully functional with desk, worktable, side chairs, and even a laptop computer.

"This is your office. Everything you need to know about Crescent Oil and Clayton's cattle business is on the laptop. You answer to no one here except me. I told everyone you are a temporary employee doing land work for Clayton. I'd appreciate it if you go along with the story."

After Dunlap had left his office, Buck sank into the chair behind the desk. Swiveling around, he gazed out the picture window at traffic moving rapidly on Northwest Expressway. From the seventh floor window, he could see the tall buildings of downtown Oklahoma City, about five miles to the south. Because of Oklahoma's prevalent winds, it has little smog and almost no air pollution. From a building as tall as Petro Place, you could see for miles.

He still hadn't opened Clayton's envelope, so he took a peek, whistling when he saw the unexpected size of his first month's check. A knock on the door interrupted his musings, and he stowed it in his pocket, turning to see the broad smile of a nice looking young man.

"You must be Buck," he said. "I'm Ty. I work in the land department."

"Hey Ty," Buck said, rising to shake his hand.

"Would you like a tour?"

"You bet," Buck said, following the young man out the door of his new office.

Ty was taller than Buck and had a full head of curly red hair. His wire-framed glasses seemed more for show than necessity as he kept them propped on his head like a tiara. He was dressed semi-casually in designer jeans and snakeskin cowboy boots, along with a dress shirt and expensive tie. Clayton obviously paid his employees well.

Crescent Oil had about forty employees. Ty introduced Buck to every one of them. It didn't take long to realize whoever did the hiring had a penchant for young, blond women, every one of them seemingly prettier than the next. Susie, the receptionist, was probably the prettiest. The title was up for grabs, and likely rested in the eyes of the beholder.

Buck met secretaries, irascible old geologists, world-weary petroleum engineers, and fast-talking landmen. Landman doesn't imply gender, as females occupying that particular job are also landmen. Ty introduced him to Dunlap's gorgeous secretary Georgia, his attraction immediate. There was not a single minority among the employees, everyone lily white. It was almost quitting time, Ty still with him when he returned to his office.

"Some of us are having drinks after work at

Nick's," the young Landman said. "We'll be in the bar."

"Thanks, maybe I'll take you up on it after I check a few things here."

Buck knew Nick's well, and his past consumption of their strong drinks had likely caused him the loss of more than a few brain cells. Ty's invitation was a good chance to glean information not available in his desktop database.

The restaurant and bar boasted the best steaks and mixed drinks in Oklahoma, its bright red wallpaper making it look like the inside of a French whorehouse. Garish wallpaper and dark surroundings were apparently conducive to good food, drinks, and conversation because the place was always brimming with happy patrons.

Ty met him at the front door and led him past the ornate bar to a couple of tables in back the regulars from Crescent Oil had pulled together. Everyone except Ty seemed preoccupied, so Buck took the opportunity to quiz the young man.

"What's the story on Roy Dunlap?"

"Mister O'Meara's best friend. Usually in here together. They go to football games and do business deals. Roy is never very far away."

"I don't recall Roy having that much money," Buck said.

"He does now. I hear Mister O'Meara lets him in on drilling deals on the ground floor. He's not hurting for money."

Buck remembered a story about Henry Ford, a person so rich he had no friends with whom to socialize. He fixed the problem by seeing to it several associates also became very wealthy. Enlightened self-interest. Perhaps it was Roy Dunlap's role.

He had little time to ponder Dunlap and Clayton as Susie the receptionist and Georgia joined them. He found himself seated between the two attractive women. Ronnie, a waitress Buck knew from the old days showed up at the table to take their drink order.

"Buck, where you been?"

"Living north of Edmond. I don't get this far south much anymore."

"You hurt my feelings. You could at least drop in occasionally."

"I'm working for a while in the building now and promise I'll be back more often."

She kissed him and then hurried away to wait on another customer. Buck noticed her long legs, highlighted by a short red velvet dress that did little to hide them. She returned with drinks for the two tables. Instead of the Coors Buck had ordered, she brought him Wild Turkey and water. Though he started to say something, the protest never left his mouth.

After drinking two strong bourbons, he sank back into the overstuffed chair. A tap on his shoulder broke the spell. It was Roy Dunlap, and he was staring an angry hole directly through him.

Georgia kissed the older man as he joined them at the table. His appearance resulted in the rapid departure of about half the people in the party. Soon, there was no one left except Ty, Susie, Roy, Georgia, and Buck.

Buck ordered chicken livers and cream gravy, a house specialty, and then excused himself to visit the little cowboy's room. When he returned, he found Ty had exchanged places with Susie and Roy Dunlap with Georgia. Just as well, he thought. He still needed to return home and feed the horses. When Ronnie arrived with yet another round of drinks, he pulled her toward him and whispered in her ear.

"Unless you intend to drive me home, I think you better replace this with a large hot coffee."

Buck knew Ronnie was married and only

flirted with customers to enhance her tips. She understood his less than cryptic message. Taking his whiskey, she smiled and kissed him, soon returning with coffee and more drinks for the rest of the party.

Buck could see that Susie and Ty, engaged in a whispered but frenetic conversation were an item. Roy Dunlap had his back to Buck and was whispering something to Georgia in which she seemed to have little interest. Ignoring Dunlap, she continued smiling at Buck.

Susie was pretty. Georgia was different, a classic beauty with Ingrid Bergman cheekbones and Marilyn Monroe eyes. Her short skirt had ridden up over her athletic thighs, either because of alcoholic indulgence or more likely by design. He only had to wonder for a moment why she was attracted to the much older Dunlap before realizing it was simply a case of *checks appeal.* Suddenly locked out of the ensuing conversations, he asked Ronnie to bring him his tab.

"You're money's no good tonight. Roy's got it covered," she said, hurrying off to wait on another table.

"Gotta go," he finally said, standing to leave.

No one protested though Georgia followed him to the door.

"We've met, although I can see you don't remember me."

Buck stared at her, dubious he had met such a gorgeous woman and forgotten about it. "Oh?" The only word he could muster.

"KK and I were roomies at OU. She introduced us in Norman one night, at a sorority party."

"That explains it," he said. "I went a while during my college years without sobering up. Still, I can't imagine forgetting you."

Georgia grinned. "See you tomorrow. I'll tell KK I saw you," she said, warming his body when she pressed her bosom against his chest.

Reeling from the effects of the bourbon, he stumbled out the door to the covered parking lot where he found the black Lincoln Navigator Clayton had provided as his company car. The big SUV was new, the sales sticker still on the back window. He didn't need to read it to know the vehicle was expensive.

A myriad of thoughts crossed his mind as he drove down Northwest Expressway. Roy Dunlap is Clayton's best friend. He is married but has a mistress who is the best friend of Kay Karson, Buck's former girlfriend and who now appears to have something going with Clayton. A plethora of possible scenarios flooded his brain as he steered the big Navigator toward Sunset Farms.

Chapter 6

The first thing Buck and Pard saw the next morning when they walked outside the barn was the black Lincoln. It seemed even larger in the sunlight. Buck grinned as he considered how he would retrieve his truck from the parking lot of the Petro Place. If nothing else, he could just leave it there until completing his job for Clayton. He had little knowledge about cattle rustling but knew someone that did. After finishing his morning chores, he gave him a call.

Buck had known Trey Calderham since high school. An investigator for the Texas and Southwestern Cattle Raisers Association, Calderham now carried a 9 mm Glock. As a special agent for both the Texas Department of Safety and the Oklahoma State Bureau of Investigation, he enjoyed full police powers in both Texas and Oklahoma and could legally arrest a cattle thief in either state if he caught one.

Trey was short, about five seven, and didn't look much like a lawman. Although the same age as Buck, he seemed older because of a prominent bald spot, hint of gray in his mustache and brown hair. The leather jacket he usually wore concealed his pistol, though he liked to flash his silver badge.

Even though they'd tangled on many occasions while growing up, Trey and Buck were friends. Despite his diminutive size, Trey could hold his own in a fight, a fact Buck had learned at an early age. The little man had remained Buck's closest friend.

Pard wasn't happy when Buck left him again with Hector because of his meeting with Calderham at Stockman's Café near the stockyards in southwest Oklahoma City. A long line of people snaked down the sidewalk, waiting to get into the popular restaurant. Trey was near the head of the line and motioned Buck to join him.

"Stockman's is too damn popular though still the best restaurant in town, at least for my money."

"Keep your money. Treat's on me today."

Trey chuckled. "Mighty big of you, seeing as you need my help and all."

"I owe you one anyway since you drove me home from Pandora's last summer."

Trey grinned, remembering the hot July night when Buck, licking his wounds because of a lost love affair, had drunk too many beers at Pandora's, a popular strip joint in Oklahoma City. At least he'd had the presence of mind to call Trey to come get him.

"You may just be more trouble than you're worth."

Buck didn't bother commenting as Wanda, a waitress who had worked at Stockman's for as long as he could remember, escorted them to a table in the back of the large and noisy restaurant.

"Need I ask, or should I just bring your regular?"

Trey nodded. "Wanda, you know me too well."

"Better make it two," Buck said.

Trey rested his elbows on the table. "I didn't realize how well you are doing."

"Huh?"

"That decked out SUV you drove up in. You can't tell me you're making that kind of money."

It was Buck's turn to grin. "Who says?"

"If so, I'm ordering a rib eye."

"Order anything you like. I'm on an expense account, and the Navigator is my company vehicle while I'm working on this case."

"Hell, maybe I should get a fifth of whiskey with my steak."

"I'll buy you two if you let me watch you drink them."

"I'm tempted to take you up on it just to show you I could. Now, what's so important?"

Buck explained Clayton's problem and finished by saying, "I don't understand why someone would risk stealing a few head of cattle."

"You checked the price of beef lately? A trailer load of cows can bring twenty grand. I'm pretty sure Clayton's cows are worth lots more."

"What'll we do?" Buck asked.

"We have inspectors working all the sale barns. They check brands, breeds, descriptions and ear tags, and send the information to our computer center in Fort Worth. If you have a description of the stolen cows, chances are we'll catch the thief."

"I have all the information on a computer database."

"Here's my email address," Trey said, handing Buck a business card. "Get me the info soon as possible. The sale of those steers may have already happened."

Wanda had returned before they had a chance to finish their conversation. "Calf fries, compliments of me and the cook."

Trey put a fork into one of the delicacies and ate it. Calf fries, breaded and fried calf testicles were the specialty of the house. The dish often gave pause to new patrons of the restaurant.

"You're a doll, Wanda," he said. "When are you going to leave your old man and marry me?"

"You couldn't handle me," she said.

Buck grinned and shook his head as Wanda disappeared into the crowd. "Do you have a new squeeze since we last talked?"

Trey drummed the side of his plate with his fork as if he had something gnawing at his insides. He finally looked Buck in the eye.

"Guess I'm gonna have to tell you sometime," he said. "Beth O'Hara and I are a couple now. We both hope you understand."

Trey's admission caught Buck by surprise. Buck and Beth, the owner of the Azure Pendant, a restaurant in Oklahoma City's Paseo District, had been a number for almost a year. Circumstances had ended their relationship, and Buck was surprised either Beth or Trey would care what his thoughts were.

"I'm happy for both of you. Though I loved her dearly, our relationship was over long ago. I can't think of anyone I would more like her to connect with."

"Thanks. I been meaning to tell you for weeks now, and you don't know how much this means to me that you understand the situation."

Buck had met Beth while on an investigation of a Cherokee artist who had met his demise at the hands of his own ex-wife. Ten years older, she fostered a persona lodged somewhere between hippy flower child and American Indian maiden. Her tousled thatch of red hair and peaches and cream complexion belied anything except Irish descent.

She had a penchant for squash blossom necklaces, dream catchers, and American Indian art. She was also an excellent chef specializing in Southwestern cuisine. Despite their age disparity, they'd enjoyed a good time line-dancing, horseback riding and making passionate afternoon love. Only Buck's roaming proclivities had caused the demise of the relationship. Now, he couldn't even remember the other woman's name.

"Who are you dating now? Maybe we can all go to dinner next week."

"Just playing the field for the past few months."

"Uh huh. I've never known you not to have two or three women on the line at any given time."

"Being broke plays hell on your love life."

"Uh huh," Trey said again.

They continued their friendly banter as they ate. Buck finally turned the conversation back to the problem at hand.

"Clayton seems to think one of his hands might be involved. At least providing information to the actual thief."

Trey nodded. "Not so farfetched. We see it all the time."

"He also suspects people living in a commune surrounded by his ranch. Know anything about it?"

Wanda had overheard Buck's question.

"Pagan lesbians," she said. "Mostly women who've worked up the nerve to leave their old men."

Trey's eyes grew wide as he listened to Wanda's description of the compound.

"Glad it's you checking them out and not me," he said when Wanda returned to the kitchen. "Hey, I hate to eat and run. I got an appointment in Piedmont at three."

"You've helped me a lot. How do you know so much about Clayton's cows?"

"He has one of the highest quality Black Angus herds in the state. His and Roy Dunlap's are tops."

"Interesting? Where is Dunlap's ranch?"

"North of Guthrie. Almost as big and fancy as

Mr. O'Meara's."

Buck pondered the possible implications of Roy Dunlap's ranch ownership as he waited outside the restaurant while Trey visited the men's room. He soon joined him, a cell phone to his ear.

"That was Beth. How about dinner at our house?"

"You two live together?"

"I'll send you the address when I acknowledge your email. Don't beg off on me or you'll miss one of the best home-cooked meals you've ever had."

"Count me in," Buck said.

Trey waved and tooled away in his red Jeep Wrangler. As Buck walked past the line of people still extending out of the restaurant, he worried about the impending dinner engagement, wondering just how awkward it would be.

Chapter 7

Buck learned, upon returning to Sunset Farms that Hector had taken to Pard, and vice versa.

"I hope he's not bothering you."

"You kidding? He's more help than another hand. Smartest dog I ever seen and he handles the horses better than me."

"I sensed a little separation anxiety when I left this morning."

Though Pard was happy to see him, he didn't protest being left behind with Hector again later the same day. When Buck pulled up to the 2nd Bank of Edmond in the new Navigator, the first person he saw was banker Jeb Stuart Johnson. The little man's mustache twitched as he watched Buck exit the luxury Lincoln.

"Get a loan from another bank?" he asked before saying hi.

"Company car," Buck said. "I'm on the payroll at Crescent Oil."

"Well then maybe now I can give you the truck loan."

"I'm just here to make a deposit."

As Buck waited at the teller's window, he realized even after catching up on his overdue bills, he had almost enough money in his account to make a down payment on a new truck. He didn't need one now. When he did, he'd already decided to take his business somewhere else. His banking finished, he pointed the Navigator toward Clayton's ranch. His conversation with Trey had spawned some questions only the wealthy oilman could answer.

Snow began falling as he drove through the open gate to Clayton's ranch. When he pulled up to the back porch, he noticed the two-seater Mercedes he was sure was KK's. He hadn't yet confronted her about her relationship with Clayton. After their meeting at the Edmond coffee shop, he realized he probably needed to. Clayton waited in the veranda's door, a glass of whiskey in his hand.

"Bout time you got here." He motioned for Buck to join him in the porch swing draped with the colorful serape. "I guess by now you heard about me and KK."

"I got no problem with it. Whatever she and I had ended long ago."

"I appreciate that."

The edge in Clayton's voice disappeared. Finishing his whiskey, he signaled Maria for another. Snowfall was picking up outside the veranda as his harried assistant brought his fresh drink.

"I had a meeting with a friend of mine that works for the Texas and Southwestern Cattle Raisers Association. I asked him to help me in the investigation. I hope it's okay with you."

"Sounds like you're making progress," Clayton said after sipping his whiskey. "Right now, I need you to visit the compound and find out for me what's going on over there."

Though Buck opened his mouth to speak, words didn't spring forth. His first month's salary still warm in his bank account, he realized whatever Clayton wanted, he also wanted.

"Okay, Boss, I'll check it out."

Clayton nodded, already knowing the power of his money. "Try to buy the property from them if you can."

"I'll do my best."

"I know you will," Clayton said, grinning. "Taking care of that little matter might work out nicely right about now, but you go when you feel like it."

It didn't take Buck long to realize Clayton's wishes were his orders. He exited the veranda with a smile and a snappy salute. It continued snowing as he returned to his car and saw someone he recognized. KK tried to ignore him. He was having none of it.

"Why are you treating me like this?" he said. "I've never done anything to hurt you."

"I really like Clayton and don't need you messing things up for me."

"Is that what this is all about?"

"I like you a lot, Buck McDivit. Clayton is different."

Snowflakes fell on his shoulders as he grabbed her arms. "Whatever we once had is over. I liked you as much as any woman I've ever known. Doesn't matter because I've moved on now."

KK's expression changed, and she hugged him. "You know I'll always love you. I've also moved on. Now Clayton's the love of my life."

"And I promise I won't do anything to change things."

"I'm so sorry," she said. "Georgia told me you are doing some work for Clayton at his oil company. I was already paranoid after what happened with her and me, and I just got a little skitsy."

"About what?"

She tugged on his hand, motioning him to sit with her in the front seat of her Mercedes.

"In case you haven't already figured it out,

Georgia is Roy Dunlap's girlfriend. I hung out with them a lot until they introduced me to Clayton. One night, I went with them to a dog fight."

"You like dog fights?"

"Not me, Roy. I think it's repulsive and so does Georgia."

"But you went anyway?"

KK nodded. "Roy's a real freak. He owns fighting dogs and roosters and bets thousands on them. I can't begin to tell you all the crazy things he's into."

"Such as?"

"He has an animal farm. You know what I mean?" Buck shook his head. "He owns a place in rural Logan County where rich spectators pay to see prostitutes have sex with animals."

"You gotta be kidding."

"I'm not, and the person who runs it for him is a man named Jimmy Quick. He does lots of other things for Roy."

"Such as?"

"You name it. He's a gorgeous man and so vain he wears a necklace with a diamond-encrusted letter Q pendant. Georgia and I decided to look him up one night when Roy and Clayton were out of town. We ended up taking him to Georgia's house."

"And now you're afraid he'll tell Roy and Clayton."

"I don't think so because Roy pays him lots of money. Still, Georgia and I got scared when we went to one of the dog fights."

"What happened?"

"Jimmy carries a big knife and cut his dog's throat with it when he lost a big fight. Buck, please don't tell any of this to Clayton. I don't think he knows how warped Roy is. I don't want him finding out because of me."

Chapter 8

Buck followed the slippery, section-line road to the entrance of the commune, shifting the Navigator into four-wheel-drive as early March snow had begun falling in heavy clumps.

Skeleton Creek split Clayton's large ranch. The commune, oddly shaped because it bounded the meandering course of the creek, wasn't far away. An oil company had graveled the road making it navigable. Barely. After passing a pumping well, he reached a barren grove of trees shrouding the pathway with leafless winter limbs. Around the bend, he got a big surprise.

There was something different about the hillside north of the bluffs. It took him a moment to realize what it was. Falling snow had abated somewhat as the scene came into focus. Dome-shaped structures protruding from the ground were actual buildings, most the size of houses, some even larger.

Partially sunken into frozen earth, the buildings seemed eerily abnormal beneath their coating of snow. Before Buck had time to reflect on the scene, a small jeep-like vehicle enclosed by a canvas top pulled up beside him. Two women, both dressed in uniforms identifying them as cops, exited the vehicle.

"Help you?" the older woman asked when he rolled down his window.

"Your neighbor, Clayton O'Meara wants to make an offer on this property. He sent me to see if you were interested."

The women exchanged glances as if they had expected him. "Come with us," one of them said.

Leaving the Navigator unlocked, he climbed into the rear seat of the strange vehicle. The two women could have passed as mother and daughter. Both had dark eyes and hair pulled back into severe buns. Neither had visible weapons, though their demeanors left little doubt they could maintain or restore order. Glancing out the window, he wondered how much snow would accumulate before morning.

The little vehicle produced no engine noise, only the silent whir of what he guessed was an electric motor. Falling snow had washed all the color from the terrain, the silence meshing with diminished tactile and aural sensations of the scenery around them.

The women drove the electric car a short distance to a dome-shaped building where they exited, motioning Buck to follow. They led him through the building's heavy oak doors where a bustle of noisy activity replaced the silence outside.

A dozen women were at work, mostly with computers. Ambient light from well-placed ceiling windows filled the room. Buck could see no light bulbs or fluorescent lighting, only the strange but effective glow from panels similar to those found in computer screens. All activity in the room ceased as Buck followed the two women down a hallway to a closed door guarded by a secretary sitting behind her desk.

"We have a messenger from O'Meara."

The young woman glanced at Buck, stood from her chair and knocked on the door. She opened it just enough to enter, shutting it behind her.

Buck waited for the two cops. Instead, they exited in the direction they had come. The young blond woman held the door open for him.

"Can I get you something to drink?"

She nodded when he said, "Coffee, black, please."

An attractive woman standing behind a lectern greeted him.

"I am Lana, chief administrator of Lykaia. How can I be of service?"

Lana was tall, every inch the match of Buck's six feet. Long, red hair draped her shoulders. A squash blossom necklace emphasizing turquoise and native silver hung from her regal neck, extending into the plunging neckline of the azure dress contrasting with her sea green eyes. Similar bracelets encircled both her wrists. Her expressive eyes, pouting lips, and figure that would have well served a super model accented a beautiful face that could launch a thousand dreams. Buck caught his breath before he spoke.

"I'm Buck McDivit. Clayton O'Meara sent me to see if you would consider an offer for your property."

Lana smiled. "If that's all you want, I'm afraid you're wasting your time. This is our home, and we don't intend to leave it."

"Can't we even talk about it?"

"Talk is cheap, Mr. McDivit."

"I've never seen anything like this place. Is there a chance someone might show me around?"

"For what reason?"

"I'll need something to tell Mr. O'Meara, why you can't bear to leave for any price."

"Maybe Mr. O'Meara should come see for himself. Meantime, I will personally give you a tour."

She didn't bother turning out the lights. As if by magic, the room darkened when his beautiful tour guide opened the door. They spent time touring the business complex and then looking at a detailed map, Lana pointing out landmarks and explaining a bit about the commune. It was already growing dark when she led him down an elaborate tunnel system lighted by the same peculiar glow as in her office.

They soon reached another building, its interior dim and atmospheric. Patrons occupied seats around cozy tables. By the aroma wafting from the rear door, he pegged the place as a restaurant. Without waiting for someone to direct them, Lana strolled to a table on a raised terrace and motioned him to join her.

"The Tiers is one of three restaurants we have here in Lykaia, this one so-called because of its terraced arrangement."

"Lykaia is a beautiful name."

"Inspired by an ancient Greek festival," she said.

Wonderful music emerging from somewhere in the dark room soon transformed Buck's thoughts to other things. When his eyes adjusted to the dimness, he realized the music was live, coming from a string quartet on a small stage. A young woman approached.

She asked, "Will you be dining with us tonight?"

Lana glanced at Buck. "Have you eaten? If you have, we can just have drinks while we talk."

"The aroma coming from the kitchen is wonderful." Lana smiled and told the waitperson they would be eating. "I'll have whatever you are having," he said.

"This is not a normal restaurant, Mr. McDivit. The menu tonight will be what everyone here eats. We grow much of our own produce, and what we don't cultivate ourselves, we trade for with neighboring farmers."

"The lighting is unusual," Buck said.

"Light emitting diodes. We burn no fossil fuels and generate electricity with a combination of solar and wind power, both of which are abundant in Oklahoma."

"The vehicle in which your officers brought me here is electric."

"We also use animal and human waste to create fuel. We make our own fuels from various plants, but just enough for our own needs."

"Your houses are passive solar."

"We partially bury our dome homes and buildings to harness the earth's natural heating and cooling properties. They all face south, and we gather the sun's energy in the winter and use reflectors to divert it in the summer. We bury our heat pumps, so their temperature remains constant, no matter what the season."

"And the tunnel system?"

"Tunnels connect all the buildings. This is for protection from the elements, safety, and convenience. Dome homes are very secure and especially safe from tornadoes and other weather phenomena quite common here in Oklahoma."

"How do your people support themselves?"

"We are doctors, lawyers, writers, artists, and musicians. We all have our talents. I have an M.B.A. from OU, which is why I am in administration. We contribute our skills to the common good."

"You don't use money?"

"Not in Lykaia, though some of us don't live here. Many of our people hold jobs in towns throughout the state. We have pooled our resources. That's how we purchased this land and paid for most of the construction. Still, we do as much bartering as we can and have alliances with other groups throughout the country, the world, and with companies and individuals we can mutually assist."

"I see," Buck said as the young woman returned with their dinner.

Expecting some vegetarian fare, ala Trey's description, he was quite delighted instead by baked tilapia, green beans, and a pilaf of rice. There was also a chilled bottle of white wine. The waitperson popped the cork and then handed it to Buck for his acceptance. Following a sip, his nod, and broad smile, she poured a glass for Lana and then topped his.

"You look surprised."

I expected everyone here to be teetotaling vegetarians," he said.

It was Lana's turn to smile. "Though we love our vegetables, most of us also eat meat. We raise tilapia here."

"Even in the winter?"

"In underground ponds, Mr. McDivit. That is the key."

"Wonderful. Your wine is very good."

"Our very own Skeleton Creek Chardonnay."

"You have a winery?"

"Oh yes. We produced our first cask last year. We have several varietals we are cultivating. The grapes grow on the slopes above the creek."

Suddenly intoxicated by Lana's beauty and the wonderful wine, Buck gazed into her limpid eyes.

"I haven't seen any men."

You noticed," Lana said. "Our commune is only for females."

"Are you . . . ?"

"Lesbians?"

Buck grinned. "It's really none of my

business."

"We are much like a microcosm of the population of the world. Some of our members are lesbians. Some are very much heterosexual. We are all here for the common good, but mostly because of our beliefs. Every citizen of Lykaia practices the same religion, Mr. McDivit. Some people call us pagans."

Buck's mouth opened wide. No words came out. Blinking once, he shook his head instead.

She stared at him and said, "No comment?"

"Except for weddings and funerals, I haven't been to church in fifteen years. At least you believe in something."

Lana seemed satisfied by his answer. She sipped her wine before asking another question.

"What about you, Mr. McDivit? You have a smooth way of eliciting information. What exactly is your line of work?"

"I was a cop for a while, and then I tried my hand as an oil and gas lease broker when oil companies began paying so well. I've done a little bounty hunting, acted as an assistant death examiner, worked from time to time for the Logan County Sheriff, and have even ridden in a few professional rodeos. I think of myself as a private investigator."

"And now you work for Mr. O'Meara?"

"For the moment," Buck said, his answer sounding a little defensive.

"Would you consider doing a job for me?"

"What do you have in mind?"

Lana tapped her fork against the table, not immediately answering his question. The string quartet continued playing in the background, Buck suddenly aware it was an old Beatle's tune.

"An outsider is harassing us. Though our police protect us, I need someone to find out who it is and determine their motivation. Someone who has a good working relationship with the Logan County Sheriff's Department in the event we need to press charges. You might fit the bill."

"Since I'm working for Mr. O'Meara, I'm afraid I have a conflict."

"We all have conflicts, Mr. McDivit. From what I can sense, you have enough integrity to overcome any possible conflict that might exist."

"I'd have to clear it with my boss first."

"I wouldn't have it any other way," she said.

Their meal finished, and the string quartet on break, the only sound as they left the restaurant was the gentle hum of electric fans.

"Can you return to Lykaia for a briefing?"

"Not until the day after tomorrow."

"Perfect. When you return, bring a change of clothes. Plan to spend two days with us. I'll explain later."

Lana's words left him with more questions than answers. The last time a beautiful female said she would explain something later he'd lost a week's wages and gained a pain which resided in his heart for almost a year.

Chapter 9

It was late when the two female police officers returned him to his Navigator. Snow covered most of the SUV's eighteen-inch wheels, though someone had cleaned his windshield. He didn't bother returning to Clayton's ranch, heading instead to his own place at Sunset Farms.

Strolling through the barn, he checked all the horses along with his own pony Lady. They were all watered, fed and seemed happy and settled for the night. Pard joined him, excited he had finally returned. As they climbed the stairs to the luxury suite, he vowed to buy Hector Ramirez a bottle of whiskey.

Buck's apartment was on the second floor of the barn, along with a half dozen other rooms, vacant now and used mostly by visiting jockeys racing at local Remington Park. His suite was finished in rare woods, polished granite, and the finest silk. It always made him feel as if he were staying in a luxury hotel in some exotic part of the world. A message from Trey Calderham was on his answering machine.

"Forget your cell phone? Call me when you get in. I got some information for you."

Buck glanced at his twenty-year-old Rolex.

After ten, it was too late to return Trey's message. He would call first thing in the morning. Right now, he was dog-tired and needed a few quality hours of sleep. Ten minutes after hitting the expensive Swedish mattress, he was already in dreamland.

Buck awoke the following morning with Pard licking his face. Fraught with too much information to process and not enough time to accomplish the task, his sleep had been fitful. Shaking off his unanswered questions, he washed his face in the marble-topped bathroom sink and then went downstairs with Pard to feed the horses.

Stirring, they awaited his caresses and gentle words. He didn't disappoint. The barn was a modern piece of architectural design constructed by Amish artisans Clayton had flown in from Pennsylvania and paid handsomely for their efforts. They had painstakingly thought out every minute detail, including an escape route in the event of a fire. Hector Ramirez liked to refer to the barn as the eighth wonder of the world.

Buck's own pony, Lady, was a quarter horse. High-spirited, she didn't like it when he failed to ride her, even for one day. Realizing as much, he patted her neck as she voiced her displeasure for not having seen him in two days. Throwing a blanket and saddle on her back, he cinched the strap and led her out of the stall toward the open door of the barn.

Snow still covered the ground, and warm breath swirled from Lady's nostrils as she started toward the road in rapt anticipation. Buck was up for the ride, having missed her as much as she had missed him. When they reached the snow-cleared county road, Pard racing behind them, he slapped her rear, propelling her forward at a breakneck clip. A half mile later, he reined in the panting pony, stretching his arms around her big neck.

"Lady, you are the only female who has ever understood me." When she whinnied and tapped her foot on the road, he added, "Maybe too well."

Buck had purposely left his cell phone in his room. When he returned, he had two missed messages, one from Trey, and the other from Clayton. He wanted to jump in the shower and luxuriate beneath warm water until he felt totally revived. Instead, he dialed Trey.

"What's up?"

"Three cows turned up at a local auction yesterday. Two were Black Angus, the third a breed no one recognized. Our agents identified them as belonging to Mr. O'Meara. There was no ear tag or lip tattoo on the strange cow, and it was too young for a brand."

"Then how could they tell it was one of Clayton's?"

"Some of our agents have judged cattle competitions at state fairs and such. They could see this cow, even though they couldn't identify the breed, was show quality and it got them to thinking something might be wrong."

"And?"

"They took a blood sample for analysis. The DNA report on the two Black Angus confirmed they were from Clayton's herd. It's just reasonable the third was also one of Mr. O'Meara's."

"Who was the seller?"

"A loser named Johnny Crabtree."

"Did they arrest him?"

"There are bigger fish to fry here. I'm emailing you the details, and don't forget about dinner tonight."

"I'll be there," Buck said before hanging up the phone, hoping Trey didn't hear the insincerity in his voice.

Buck owed Clayton a call but decided his shower couldn't wait. Stripping down, he stepped beneath cascading water in Mrs. O'Meara's world-class shower, finished in Italian marble and big enough for a half dozen good friends.

As warm water sprayed his shoulders, he couldn't keep his imagination from concocting fantasies about the beautiful Lana and her long red hair. Maybe she wanted him to spend the night so he could satisfy her own fantasy about him. When water streamed cold in the shower, he realized it was probably not the case.

Like water in the hot and steamy shower, his fantasy quickly cooled. The daydream, no matter how improbable, was imprudent because, technically, he was now her employee, assuming Clayton didn't protest. He plopped down into an overstuffed chair, so comfortable he had trouble getting out of it whenever he sat in it. Finally dragging away from its grasp, he called Clayton.

"Tell me about your visit to the commune."

"There are a couple hundred people there, and they have all combined their assets. From the look of the expensive and complex technology they've put into place, I'd say they are more able to buy you out than vice versa."

There was silence on the phone for a long moment.

"That's not what I wanted to hear," Clayton finally said.

"Don't shoot me, I'm only the messenger."

"It ain't over yet," Clayton said. "Information is power. I want you to go back and get as much as possible.

"No problem. They want to hire me to do some investigative work for them. I thought I better pass it by you before I accepted."

"Sounds like a perfect opportunity to spy on them for me."

"I don't spy on people I'm working for," Buck said

"Don't get your panties in a wad," Clayton said, "I wasn't suggesting you stab anyone in the back."

"They seem willing to tell me everything I want to know. Lana, the woman who runs the place, issued you an invitation to check out things for yourself."

"Oh yeah?"

"You ought to go just to see her. A real looker."

"What else?"

"Have you heard of a man named Johnny Crabtree?"

"Worked here on the ranch a time or two. Look, Buck, I have to go now. We'll talk about this later," Clayton said, hanging up the phone.

"Damn it!" Buck said. "Working for that man is like beating yourself in the head with a ball-peen hammer."

Chores completed and feeling considerably better, he said goodbye to Pard and headed for town. He'd decided to spend the day reading every entry in the computer database until he had a better picture of Clayton's cattle operation. He didn't know what he would accomplish by revisiting Lykaia, though he looked forward to seeing gorgeous Lana again. Susie met him at the front door.

"We missed you last night."

"Working late."

"Anybody I know?" she asked.

"Don't know. Ever hear of a commune in Logan County called Lycaia?"

"I remember hearing Georgia say something about it," she said.

"Oh, like what?" he said.

"Had a little bit too much to drink that night and I can't really remember. Gotta get back to work. Catch you later."

Buck watched her hurry away down the hall before heading to his office. Shutting the door behind him, he pulled up the database of Clayton's cattle operation, soon finding what he was looking for. Clayton's supervisor, Garth Dunlap was the man responsible for periodically hiring Johnny Crabtree.

"Dunlap?" Buck said as someone opened his door.

"Yes?"

Buck glanced up to see buttoned-down Roy Dunlap. "Do you know someone named Garth Dunlap?"

"My little brother, a perennial ne'er-do-well. Clayton was kind enough to give him a job."

Dunlap nodded when Buck said, "Clayton's foreman?"

"What's he done now?"

"Nothing; I was just reading Clayton's employee list and wondered if you two are related."

"Garth was a change of life baby for my parents. I had already graduated high school when he was born. We were never close."

Buck glanced out the big picture window at traffic streaming past on Northwest Expressway, not wanting Roy Dunlap to know how interested he really was in his younger brother. When Dunlap left his office, he continued scanning files, stopping only briefly to order lunch from Nick's. It was five when he finally glanced at his watch.

Turning off the laptop, he thought about his impending dinner date with Trey and his former girlfriend, Beth O'Hara. He hadn't seen her since their breakup and had only talked to her once on the phone. She had made several, probably very true though still uncomplimentary remarks about him. Her words continued to plague his thoughts.

He wasn't looking forward to seeing Miss O'Hara, and he didn't want to hurt Trey's feelings. His thoughts drifted to his short time with Beth as he pointed the Navigator toward the Paseo,

Oklahoma City's old art district. She had a restaurant, the Azure Pendant, where they'd first met. Before reaching the Paseo, he reflected on what Susie had said and made a mental note to ask Georgia what she knew about Lycaia.

Chapter 10

Although not far from Petro Place, The Paseo District occupied a much older part of town. A big Oklahoma sky had grown dark as Buck cruised through the cemetery north of the Paseo and entered the little art district.

A diamond in the rough, the area waited patiently for the next real estate boom. It reminded him of Santa Fe with its stucco buildings painted pink and garish blue. There were a couple of restaurants, a few nightclubs, a head shop, several art studios, and little else. Beth's restaurant was the most popular establishment in the Paseo.

Her manager was running the place tonight, something that never happened when he was dating her. Stymied by her workaholic tendencies, he'd often found himself wishing during their brief relationship the restaurant would catch fire and burn to the ground.

When he'd dated Beth, she'd lived in the second story of a tiny apartment in a complex located west of the restaurant. Trey had somehow convinced her to move to new digs, although still located in the Paseo. He had purchased a two-story building, once the office of a group of eclectic architects. Buck looked forward to inspecting it, even as he worried about his meeting with her.

When he'd first met Beth, she'd seemed everything he ever wanted in a woman. Later, he realized she was probably everything he ever needed in a mother. The thought confounded him and left their relationship in shambles. Parking on the street beside Trey's flame red Jeep Wrangler, he strolled to the door.

"Come on in this place, Cowboy," Trey said, opening the blond oak and cut glass door almost before Buck had time to ring the bell.

The new abode was everything Buck had imagined and more. Trey led him through an entryway, to a living area painted in earth tones and decorated with American Indian art. In addition to the paintings, antique Indian blankets graced the walls.

"We could have bought a Mercedes for what I paid for that one," Trey said, pointing at an Indian blanket mounted like a piece of art.

"It's quite old and worth every penny," a feminine voice said from behind.

It was Beth, dressed much the same as the first time Buck had met her, in a faux buckskin dress and an azure feather in her raven-red hair. She was smiling, so he hugged her.

At least ten years older, she was one of those lucky people who never seemed to age. Not beautiful in the classic sense, she exuded sex. He held on to her for a moment too long, his hands remembering the softness and warmth of her shoulders, her red hair reminding him of Lana.

"Ahem," Trey said, clearing his throat.

"Sorry," Buck said, pulling away from her. "Guess I had forgotten just how gorgeous Beth is. I never could keep my hands off her. You are a lucky man, Trey."

"I'm the lucky one," Beth said, giving Buck a chance to wipe the silly grin off his face. "Trey's the best man I ever met."

"Ouch!" Buck said.

"That's why I love her," Trey said. "Let us show you the rest of the place."

Once a large open studio, Trey, and Beth had converted the space into a gorgeous apartment. The two-storied building had a wonderful view from its large open balcony overlooking the Paseo. Trey and Buck relaxed on a sofa draped with a bright red Navajo rug, and Beth brought them cold mugs of beer.

"You two have things to talk about," she said. "I'll be in the kitchen and will let you know when dinner is ready."

"Great view and so relaxing," Buck said. "If I lived here, I'd never get anything done."

Trey sipped his beer and nodded. "She likes you a lot."

"I like her. Good thing for you that we broke up."

"She's my dream woman," Trey said.

The beer's alcoholic effect quickly began acting on Buck. "Is this a strong brew I'm drinking?"

"I visit Fort Worth every week or so and always return with a case or two."

Oklahoma's strange liquor laws had resulted in big beer companies refusing to sell only three-point-two beer in the state. The beer Buck was drinking had considerably more alcohol, and he felt his cheeks grow progressively warmer.

"Something bothers me. What makes Clayton's cows so unique?"

"How much do you know about cattle?"

Trey chuckled when Buck answered, "T-bone, medium rare."

"There are maybe eight hundred breeds of

cattle divided roughly between cold and hot climate varieties. Ranchers want a breed that has few calving problems and consistently produces quality beef. There are around fifty common cattle breeds in the United States."

"Like Black Angus?"

"Oklahoma is an unusual state weather wise. A valuable breed is one that can survive our cold winters, hot summers and maintain consistent qualities."

"You think Clayton has developed such a breed?"

"That's the rumor on the street. Clayton's cows supposedly thrive in Oklahoma and have the qualities our breeder's desire. The cow Crabtree sold in the auction might qualify as a new breed."

"How would you know?"

"I guess we'd have to see a bunch of cows with similar traits."

"What is something like developing a new breed worth?"

"I can't count that high. To make the finances work, the breeder has to control access to his stock. Other breeders pay license fees for the right to raise the cattle and form associations to protect their rights."

"You know something else, don't you?"

Trey sipped his beer before answering. "The DNA sample of the unusual cow Crabtree sold indicates it's a variety of cattle none of us has ever seen before."

Buck had to think a moment about the implications of what Trey had just told him.

"If someone stole a truckload of cows, why did they only try to sell three of them?"

"Don't know for sure. I do have a theory."

"Which is?"

"Say three men were hired to perform the actual theft. Maybe they stole an extra three cows to sell and split the proceeds, not telling the person that hired them. The three extras they took were Black Angus, but they wouldn't all fit in their stock trailer. In confusion, they probably shooed away an Angus. Being short, they sold one of the special breed cows instead at the auction."

"Then you think the cattle thieves were working for someone else."

Trey nodded. "Someone who badly wanted a sample of Clayton's new breed."

People were milling on the street below, moving slowly between clubs. Music wafted up from the nightspots, filling the early spring night with sounds of jazz and salsa music. The temperature was in the fifties, much milder than the previous day when snow covered the ground. Mostly melted now, there was still a nip of winter in the air, though not enough to keep Trey and Buck, and the revelers below from enjoying a wonderful late March evening.

"Tell me about Johnny Crabtree," Buck finally said.

"A real piece of work. Lives in a trailer house northwest of Crescent in a little community of like-minded people."

"Oh?"

"Redneck racists with larceny in their veins, linked to everything from home invasions to crystal meth, and probably everything in between."

"So Crabtree had two partners."

"Yes, and all three were working for someone else. Someone smarter than Crabtree. You can bet good money on it."

Peeking out the door, Beth interrupted their discussion. "Dinner is ready."

They followed her inside, Buck's senses aroused by the aroma drifting from the kitchen. Beth seated them at a table in a cozy nook and then began serving dinner. As Buck savored his first bite, he remembered one of the reasons he liked her so much.

"This is wonderful."

"Roast pork loin with red chile peanut mole. It's my variation of a recipe I picked up in New Mexico."

Trey and Beth laughed when Buck said, "I might just have to fistfight you for Beth before the night's over."

When their laughter abated, she said, "Trey tells me you visited Lykaia, the Southern Death Cult Commune."

Buck did a double take "I don't have a clue what you mean by Southern Death Cult."

"One of the oldest Native American sites in the U.S. is the Spiro Mounds in southeastern Oklahoma. The Mounds were a spiritual complex for the Southern Death Cult, a Native American religion. The Lykaians practice a modern form of this very old religion."

"You just told me something I didn't know," Trey said.

"I thought you were an expert on everything about Oklahoma."

"Maybe when it comes to cows. How do you know so much about the compound?"

"Their bank lent me the money to buy the Azure Pendant," Beth said.

"They have a bank?"

"Yes, though they only do business with, well, women."

"How did you find out about it?"

"You boys never have trouble getting anything you need, at least when it comes to business. It's not as easy for a woman. Word gets around."

"Are they lesbians?" Trey asked.

"Why would you even ask that question? Women usually live longer, not to mention husbands often leave their wives for someone younger. The group looks out for each other when there's not a man around to satisfy the role."

Trey gave her a sad puppy look. "That's not the way you feel about me, is it?"

"Like I said, you're the best man I've ever known. Far better than my first husband who left me stranded after I followed him here from Texas. You know I love you."

"I guess I know now how you felt about me," Buck said with a grin, trying to impart a little levity back into the conversation.

It worked because Beth laughed and Trey guffawed, almost choking on his beer.

"You know what I mean," Beth said. "Women sometimes need other women. Just like you two need each other from time to time."

Talk of the compound erased the smile from Trey's face, and he began eating his red chile peanut mole.

"This is wonderful, and your exes really were brainless."

It was true Beth could cook like no other. It wasn't the most important quality Buck had liked about her. Nor was it sex, although she left him with no complaints in that particular category.

She had an opinion on most everything, one she had thought out and not just thought up. Buck missed calling her for advice and hearing her opinions. Halfway through the mole, he realized he was only a disappearing blip on her radar screen.

Chapter 11

It was late when Buck made it home to Sunset Farms. Hector was awake, whittling a chunk of wood as he sat on the porch of his house. Pard was with him and licked his face when he joined them on the steps.

"You're up late. What's going on?"

"I stayed up to tell you a man dropped by tonight."

"What did he want?"

"You."

Hector was not an impulsive man. Something had spooked him.

"He asked how long I had known you and what you do for a living. I didn't know if he was a bill collector or what, so I didn't tell him much. Just enough to get him to leave."

"Did he say his name?"

"He said I didn't need to know who he was."

"What did he look like?"

"A big man, six four or so, dressed in expensive jeans and boots. He wore lots of jewelry, a fancy watch, rings, and a heavy gold necklace with a dangling letter."

"What letter?"

Hector had a stick in his hand and used it to trace the letter Q in the dirt in front of them.

The late night visit by the mysterious man worried Buck as much as it had spooked Hector and LaDona, so he contacted his employer, Virginia O'Meara. An intensely private person, she immediately hired a local security firm to patrol the premises on a regular basis.

Following his talk with Trey, he had new questions for Clayton. The day seemed like spring, the sky blue, and sunny as he headed toward Clayton's ranch. Pard wanted to come along but seemed to understand when Buck told him he needed to guard LaDona and the baby. Since Clayton wasn't expecting him, the guards detained him at the gate, harassing him unmercifully, as usual. It didn't matter because a call to the boss got the doors opened for him.

Buck parked outside the veranda and entered through the back door without knocking. He found a smiling Clayton sitting in his rocking chair, a ubiquitous glass of whiskey in his hand.

"You're up mighty early today."

It was Buck's turn to grin. "It's you who likes to sleep until eight every morning."

"Only when I got a good reason," Clayton said, glancing at his bedroom curtains.

"More power to you. KK was too much woman for me."

"You're really not mad at me because of her, are you?"

"We broke up long ago. I'm happy she landed with someone as stable as you are, and you're lucky because she's one hot woman."

"You don't have any doubts I can handle her, do you?"

Buck grinned again. "If you can, then you're a better man than I am." Outside, Clayton's hands were hurrying about as if something important had happened. "What's up?"

"Nothing really," Clayton said.

There was a tacit hint in Clayton's abbreviated explanation that told Buck he was covering something up.

"We're on the same side here."

All signs of Clayton's smile had disappeared. "We had another little robbery last night."

"And you were going to keep it from me?"

Clayton squirmed in his rocker. "There are things about my cattle operation we haven't discussed."

"Like your secret breed that you didn't bother telling me about?"

Clayton glanced around the veranda to see if anyone was listening to the conversation.

"How do you know about that?"

"Trey told me."

Clayton motioned for Buck to follow him into the house.

"Walls have ears. There are certain things I only discuss in the privacy of my office."

Clayton's ranch house was huge and expensively decorated. Buck followed him down a teak-floored hallway, its walls lined with expensive paintings of different cattle breeds. Clayton finally stopped at a closed door equipped with a combination lock below the knob. Standing in front of the lock so neither Buck nor anyone else could see, he worked the combination and opened the door.

Clayton led him into a large room with no windows, motioning him to sit in an overstuffed leather chair while he locked the door. He sat in his own leather chair behind the largest desk Buck had ever seen. The woodwork was so intricate it likely cost a small fortune. Gazing around the room, he took in the paraphernalia Clayton had probably spent a lifetime collecting.

Much like the paintings in the hallway, cattle pictures occupied much of the wall space. There were also pictures of Clayton with many former presidents—both of the Bush's, and a much younger Clayton with his arm around Ronald Reagan. There was no sound from outside the room.

"This office is secure. The only place on this ranch that is. We can talk straight here. Want something to drink?"

"Coffee sounds good."

Clayton made a face before punching a button on his desk phone. "Maria, bring us some coffee." Without waiting for an answer, he replaced the receiver. Leaning on his elbows as he clasped his hands, he said, "Now tell me what you know about my cattle operation."

"Trey's people took DNA from a cow they were suspicious of at a sale barn. One of your cows. It wasn't a breed they were familiar with. Trey thinks you may be developing a new breed. Is it true?"

"Damn it! I've spent a million bucks trying to keep my operation quiet. Now everyone in central Oklahoma knows what I'm up to."

"Someone seems to know all about your new breed, and it may be the very reason you are losing cows. You need to tell me, so we'll be on the same page."

Clayton took a healthy slug of his whiskey before answering. "My cows are bred specifically for Oklahoma and Texas. The best cow ever produced for this region."

"What's something like that worth?"

"Ten times more than I ever made in the oil business."

"Then your secret is damn sure worth stealing. Did you know Roy Dunlap is into dog and chicken fighting?"

"What he does on his own time is his

business."

"Maybe it's not as pretty as you think. Some of the things he's into stink to high heaven. A man named Jimmy Quick does most of his dirty work."

"What's this got to do with my cows?"

"Mr. Quick paid a visit to Sunset Farms last night, asking Hector and LaDona lots of questions about my background and my relationship with you."

"What are you getting at?"

"Only one person, Roy Dunlap, could have put him up to it. Maybe we flushed that covey of quail we were talking about."

Clayton's hand relaxed, and he smiled again. "I knew I picked the right man when I hired you. Then again, maybe you are way off base. Maybe those women over at the commune are doing the stealing."

"I can't agree with your paranoia. If they are, I will find out about it."

Clayton pointed his finger at Buck. "Just git 'er done!" They were both laughing and walking out the door as Maria arrived with Buck's coffee. "We're finished in here. Bring it out to the veranda."

Buck followed Clayton as he hurried down the hallway. "You treat her like shit. Haven't you ever heard of please and thank you?"

"Women like to be told what to do. It's their lot in life."

Buck glanced up at the ceiling. "I hope your roof is lightning-proof."

Clayton watched as Buck walked down the short flight of stairs to the Navigator.

"What's on your dance card now?" he asked.

"On my way to the commune."

"Good," Clayton said. "I set the sheriff on them just for general principles. He should already be there."

It bothered Buck that Clayton had called the sheriff and pointed a guilty finger at the women of Lykaia. He seriously doubted they were involved in any way. He also wondered why Lana wanted him to spend the night. His curiosity overflowing, he'd brought a change of clothes and had asked Hector to feed the horses and Pard while he was gone.

The roads were clear since the last time he'd visited. Unpaved roads in Logan County can become very slippery following rain or snow as he had experienced on more than one occasion. Today, because of the sunshine and a steady breeze, he had no trouble tooling down the steep and narrow dirt road leading to the compound.

New oil well lease signs marked both sides of the road, attesting to drilling activity instigated by rising oil prices. Suddenly flush financially, he thought about asking Clayton to let him take a small interest in a well. As he mulled the idea, the front bumper of a police cruiser appeared from around a corner. It was the Logan County sheriff.

Sheriff Hagen, probably in his mid-fifties, had employed him more than once when he needed an extra deputy or someone to help the death investigator inspect a crime scene. Buck stopped on the side of the road and waited for him to pull alongside. Seeing the Navigator, Hagen parked the dark blue Dodge Charger in front of it.

Two inches shorter than Buck, Hagen had short-cropped black hair and a mustache. A former Army officer, he didn't like wearing uniforms. The badge, prominently displayed on his belt, was the only indication he was the most powerful law officer in Logan County.

"What are you up to?" Buck asked when the sheriff stepped out of the car.

"Chasing cattle thieves. Got any in the back of that pussy wagon of yours?"

Sheriff Hagen had a dry wit and rarely cracked a smile. Buck realized he was enjoying his little joke.

"If I did, I wouldn't be stopping on the side of the road to chit-chat with the county sheriff, now would I, Sheriff?"

"Guess not. Can't say as much for some of the genetic defects living around here. We busted a meth house about a block from the station last week."

Buck and Sheriff Hagen both knew the use of crystal meth always resulted in diminished mental capacity, often making users and dealers their own worst enemies.

"I was just over at Clayton's. He said you would be checking out the compound to see if the women there stole his cattle."

Hagen tapped the hood of the car. "Clayton's my biggest political contributor. Whenever he asks me to check something out, I do it, no matter how stupid the request."

"They don't strike me as criminal types."

"Right about that. I meant to stop by, anyway. Someone's been harassing them. Mostly petty stuff though it could get serious if we don't do something about it."

Buck's ears perked. "What sort of stuff?"

"Someone running around naked, harassing the women."

"Any ideas?"

"The usual suspects. Take a look." Sheriff Hagen rolled out a topographic map on the hood of the Charger. "Skeleton Creek runs right through Clayton's and the compound's property. There is a group of inbreeds and dope freaks living up the road, on the other side of Crescent. Whenever something like this happens, you can almost bet they're involved."

"Trey mentioned the place. Can you pin the

theft of Clayton's cows on them?"

"I'm working on it."

"Two women in uniform stopped me at the gate last time I visited the commune," Buck said.

"They have their own security people, and do a pretty capable job. Still, I don't want a rape occurring over there."

Buck continued looking at the topo map. The Sheriff had oriented it, so it faced north.

"There's no fence line between Clayton's place and the compound," he said. "Whoever stole the cows probably ran them into the creek. The bottom is wide and flat and mostly hidden by blackjacks growing on both sides. Unless I miss my guess, they herded them to an oil lease, loaded them into a trailer, and took off with them."

Buck traced the course of Skeleton Creek with his index finger. "They probably went west, the direction of the nearest paved road. They could have gone anywhere once they reached Highway 74."

"Possibly to another county, outside my jurisdiction. Professional thieves know how to work the system."

"A flawed system," Buck said. "What'll we do?"

"Ask your buddy, Trey. He has the authority, no matter what county, or state, is involved."

"Trey said Roy Dunlap's ranch is north of Crescent. Is it near the biker community?"

Sheriff Hagen nodded. "Practically adjacent to one another. Why do you ask?"

Buck continued staring at Sheriff Hagen's topo map. "Just trying to get my bearings."

"Keep it," Hagen said. "I've got a dozen more back at the office."

Buck saluted as Sheriff Hagen shut the door of the Logan County police cruiser behind him.

"Thanks, Sheriff," he said.

Hagen pointed his finger at Buck. "Stay out of

trouble. I'm friends with the sheriffs of Payne, Lincoln, and Oklahoma Counties. You're out of luck if you get in trouble somewhere else."

"I'll do my best," Buck said.

He watched Hagen drive away down the section line road. Placing the topo map on the hood of his own truck, he glanced at it again. Skeleton Creek lay just over the hill, and he made a mental note to return, maybe with Lady, and follow the creek to see where it led.

Chapter 12

Although he didn't know why Lana wanted him to spend the night at Lykaia, he continued to maintain his fantasies about her possible intentions. He was thinking about it when the Lykaia police met him at the gate. They exchanged a few meaningless words as they collected his bag, abandoned the Navigator, and proceeded to the main compound in their electric vehicle.

The two female officers escorted him to the concourse of tunnels beneath the commune, soon reaching an area resembling a hotel lobby. They pointed him to an attractive young woman standing behind what appeared to be a check-in counter.

"She'll take care of you from here."

Buck introduced himself to the smiling woman behind the counter.

"Of course, Mr. McDivit. Your room is ready and here is your key. Make yourself at home, and someone will summon you later."

She handed him a plastic card with a magnetic strip and pointed him down the hall. As he keyed the door and entered, he wondered just how big the hotel was, and how many guests they usually had—a question he intended to ask Lana at the appropriate time.

Unlike any other hotel he had stayed in, this one had dim green lighting that flooded the interior with an ethereal glow. He sprawled on the bed, falling asleep and not waking until a knock on the door interrupted his vivid dream. Rubbing his eyes, he opened the door and stared at a friendly young woman, her hand extended in a business-like fashion.

"I'm Kristy. I'll be your guide tonight."

She was young, probably in her early twenties. Dark expressive eyes matched her raven hair and olive complexion and highlighted teeth good enough for a toothpaste commercial. She followed him into the room, waiting while he stepped into the bathroom and returned with combed hair and a fresh shirt.

"What now?" he asked.

"You'll soon find out," she said, as he followed her down a long hallway.

They reached the restaurant he recognized as the same one he and Lana had dined the first night he'd visited Lykaia. This time, Kristy left him alone at a table with a chilled bottle of Skeleton Creek Cabernet.

Wondering about all the intrigue, he dined to the dulcet chords of the same string quartet as before, feeling euphoric after his first glass of wine. A half-hour had passed before Kristy joined him, occupying the chair across the candle-lit table from him.

"You're going to take part in a ceremony tonight."

"Lana didn't mention anything about a ceremony. I thought I was here to do some investigative work for her."

"I don't question Lana's intentions, and I'm sure she has her reasons."

Underground for several hours, Buck had lost track of time and wondered if it was also part of Lana's intentions. Strangely affected by the wine, it didn't seem to matter to him.

He followed Kristy back down the underground hallway to an opening leading to the surface. When they exited the tunnel system, he realized just how much the underground experience and wine had confused his psyche. The sky was dark, the day growing late.

Kristy led him through the starless darkness for some distance, finally reaching an Indian teepee. She held the flap for him, waiting as he entered. A small fire burned in the center of the teepee, smoke rising upward and disappearing through an opening high above them. Feeling more than a bit detached from reality, he sensed he had imbibed something stronger than just wine. Whatever it was had elevated his euphoria and prevented him from caring.

"Take off your clothes and put on this breechcloth."

She handed him a deerskin breechcloth and waited, not bothering to leave the tent.

"Well?" he said.

"Well, what?"

"Aren't you going to give me some privacy while I change?"

She laughed. "Get used to it. There'll be lots of eyes on you before the night's over."

Kristy waited with her arms crossed, watching him with a half smile on her pretty face as he undressed. In his state of unexplained elation, he didn't mind, even enjoying her voyeurism.

"We're not done. I need to paint you," she said after he'd donned the breechcloth.

Buck sat on the stool, half-naked as Kristy painted his face and chest with ancient symbols whose meaning perhaps only she knew. When she finished, he looked like an Indian warrior, complete with war paint and ceremonial feathers. Pleased with her handiwork, Kristy flashed him a smile and then kissed him.

"What now?"

"Showtime," she said, grabbing his hand and leading him to the door of the teepee.

Snow and inclement weather of the previous week had vanished. Goosebumps still popped up on his skin as they followed the moonlit trail toward percussive drumming of Indian tom-toms. They soon reached a clearing in the forest, a large bonfire burning, and a hundred or more people, all women, sitting or standing around the fire.

Only feathers and animal pelts clothed the mass of chanting females. Like Buck, colorful paints decorated their faces and exposed skin. Kristy escorted him to a small group of women, their extra feathers, and adornments marking them as leaders. He also noticed someone he recognized. It was Georgia. She blew him a kiss as Kristy redirected his attention with a shove of the shoulder.

The most ornate female, he noted, was Lana, looking nothing like the corporate executive of their last meeting. She didn't speak when he stood before her, simply nodding for him to sit on the colorful serape draped on the ground beside her.

Waves of frenzied dancers moved into the circle, he observed with only the giddiest of perception. When offered, he drank from a cup passed around the circle, almost instantly feeling intoxicated. The drink numbed him and he, like the women around him, began swaying to the tom-tom's hypnotic rhythm. The drumming continued as half-naked women danced in and out of the circle. When Lana handed him a ceremonial pipe, he took a puff without thinking, psychedelic smoke rushing straight to his brain.

As the beat grew louder, dancing became ever more frenetic and sensual. Even in his drugged state, he realized he was participating in an ancient revel that had some intense meaning to the women dancing in and out of the circle lighted only by the center bonfire and the moon and stars.

A stunning woman soon joined the other dancers. Tall, with long black hair extending to the crack of her well-turned derriere, she wore only a breechcloth, paint, and feathers. The strange and intricate tattoo on her left shoulder blade, a pair of intertwined rattlesnakes with strange heads, only added to her exotic beauty.

Even in his extreme state of drug-induced euphoria, his mind did a double take. The woman carried a large rattlesnake, this one alive. Despite his mental condition, his eyes riveted on her erect nipples and the snake.

She danced to a spot directly in front of him, thrusting the writhing reptile high into the air. Slowly, she lowered it, until its head resided directly in front of him. Zoned almost totally out, he stared into the viper's eyes as it jutted its pointed tongue a few inches from his face.

Whatever drug had invaded his brain had also removed any fear or anxiety about the reptile's danger. Like star-crossed lovers, they exchanged a kiss that would have curdled his blood. If he were cognizant, which he wasn't. The gorgeous woman released the serpent, and it slithered away, into the darkness.

Prompted by some primeval urge, he stood from the serape and waded into the circle crowded again with chanting dancers, arms stretched to the sky, reveling in the proximity to so many half-naked females, his senses flooded by sound and the musky odor of burning wood and sweating bodies.

Women danced shoulder to shoulder, Buck among them. In his impaired state of mind, he watched Lana, dancing half-naked and enjoying herself immensely. He forgot the images of Lana and the other women, focusing instead on the drumming beat of Indian tom-toms and dozens of wildly chanting women. The revel continued through the night.

Chapter 13

As a brilliant Oklahoma dawn greeted the eastern sky, the drumming and dancing ceased, and all the women prostrated themselves on the ground. Soon, they were rolling in the dirt, laughing, and carrying on. Dust, kicked up by hours of frenzied dancing, covered their perspiring bodies.

The frenzy ended when one of the dirt-coated women tore off her skimpy outfit and ran naked into the woods. Even coated with dust and dirt, Buck could see it was Lana. The other women ripped off their clothing and followed her. Caught up in the moment, he did the same. Lana led them to a large pond and completed a running dive off the wooden dock.

Buck and the women jumped in after her, the pond soon filled with naked females, laughing and squealing, water still icy after the recent snow. Cold water filled his spirit with feelings of revival and well-being. After washing sand and dirt off his skin and out of his hair and eyes, he followed the women as they began exiting the pond.

They moved down the trail, back toward Lykaia, this time at a much easier pace. None of them seemed to notice Buck or care he was as naked as they were. They departed the woods and into a recreational park where people met them with warm terry cloth robes. Temperatures were in the fifties and the robe felt snug and comfortable after the chilly dip in the pond.

A feast waited on picnic tables, and Buck realized just how famished he was following the night long revel. Kristy found him in the crowd, grabbed his arm, and led him to an empty seat next to Lana. She had a mouth filled with melon and motioned him to help himself to the virtual cornucopia of food on the table in front of them. He didn't need prompting.

The feast consisted of fruit, vegetables, juices, and meat—everything probably grown on the compound or bartered from neighboring farms. Everyone was apparently as hungry as he was, doing lots of eating and little talking. Lana finally dropped her knife and smiled at him.

"You survived the revel," she said.

"Yes, at least I think so. Do you do this often?"

When she shook her head, her crimson hair rippled in the sun.

"Last night marked the spring equinox. We celebrate the beginning of spring and give thanks for the bounty of the earth."

"I couldn't help but notice I'm the only male present."

"Because you were chosen," she said.

"Chosen?"

"To perform an important and integral religious role in our spring equinox revel."

"Please enlighten me," he said.

"Last night you performed the role of Fertility Deity in our ritual. Thanks to you, the women of Lykaia will be healthy and fertile this year."

Buck's mouth opened slightly. "I thought you asked me here to assist you in an investigation."

Lana touched his hand. "You aren't offended, are you?"

"You didn't have to drug me. You could have just asked."

Still holding his hand, Lana squeezed. "There is no duplicity here. We all felt the same potency of the ceremonial drugs we use in our religion."

"I thought you were pagans."

"What I said was some people think of us as pagans, though that's not what we are."

"Last night's revel seemed more than just a little paganistic," he said.

"All religions have their roots in paganism," she said.

"I'm no expert on religion. Maybe you'd better explain."

"Easter has no set date. It's determined by the cycles of the moon. The name Easter came from Eostre the Goddess of Fertility. Each year the children hunt eggs, a universal female symbol. Christmas began as a mid-winter celebration. Scandinavian pagans called the holiday Yule, a word now synonymous with Christmas. Shall I continue?"

"I didn't mean anything negative by my comment," he said.

"We actually consider our religion more closely aligned with early Native Americans."

"Like the Southern Death Cult?"

"You have done your homework. Our religion celebrates the earth. We are but occupants of the universe. We do our best never to take more than we return in kind. It's a simple concept. One we believe is important."

"You said there's no duplicity in Lycaia. Now you tell me my participation in the revel was the only reason you wanted me here."

Lana closed her eyes a moment. "I tricked you, and I apologize. I only did it because I didn't think you would otherwise agree to serve our purpose in the revel."

"Then there's no intruder harassing the commune?"

"No. Someone murdered the person chosen to act as Fertility Deity this year. There was no time to prepare someone else."

"You mean Frank Boggs?" Buck asked.

Lana nodded. "The Fertility Deity can't be just any man. He must be young, virile and athletic, three qualities that you possess. I'm sorry I tricked you."

"Then maybe I should leave now," he said.

Lana grabbed his wrist, looking disturbed as she stared into his eyes.

"We need you to perform one more task before you do that."

"I don't know," he said. "This is all a little too confusing to me."

"You said Mr. O'Meara would like to make an offer on our property. If you'll stay and complete your role, then we'll consider his offer."

"You tricked me once. How do I know that this isn't a trick?"

"You don't, though I'm sure your employer won't be happy if he learns you could have possibly negotiated a sale of our property but decided against it for personal reasons."

Buck blinked, and then his serious expression dissolved into a droll smile.

"You're good, you know it?" he said.

"Then you'll stay and assist us in completing the ritual?"

"Maybe, if you'll at least tell me exactly what you expect me to do?"

"Nothing that will cause you bodily harm, or coerce you into harming someone else. On that, you have my word."

"Then you leave me with no choice. What

next?"

Lana glanced up at the flock of geese, honking and raising a ruckus as they winged overhead on their way south.

"Esme is our spiritual advisor. From this point on she will instruct and guide you through the remainder of the ceremony."

Lana grinned when Buck said, "Then I'm at your service."

When a young woman joined them, it became apparent to Buck the two women were a couple. His fantasies of a possible romantic relationship with the redheaded beauty flew out the window. Following a more-than-friendly hug and kiss, she introduced the woman to him.

"This is Sara. We have an appointment. Kristy will take you to see Esme."

Kristy took Buck to the hotel room where he slept, recovering from the all-night revel, until she returned for him. When they exited the underground complex, he was surprised that it was already after dark. Solar lamps lighted the narrow pathway they followed into the woods. Lights soon disappeared. It didn't matter because Kristy apparently knew the way.

It wasn't far to the small clearing occupied by the same large buckskin teepee he had used as a dressing room the previous night. Kristy opened the flap, entering without verbally acknowledging their arrival. Lit by a small fire and a few candles, the inside of the teepee shined with an ephemeral glow, a woman Buck instantly recognized waiting in the dim light for them.

"I'm Buck McDivit."

She didn't bother shaking his hand. After a pregnant pause, he just stood there, waiting for her response, good or bad.

"You're a handsome man, even with all your

clothes on," she finally said.

"Thanks," Buck said. "At least I guess."

"I am Esme, high-priestess of Lykaia."

Esme was the beautiful woman with the rattlesnake tattoo who danced nearly naked during the ceremony. As he stood close enough to touch her, he felt his skin grow warm. The sensation passed up from his loins to his neck. His face felt as if it had turned red. When she smiled, he was sure of it.

A sound behind him, the low growl of an animal that was not quite a dog, caused the hair to stand up on the back of his neck. Turning his head, he saw the bared fangs of a large beast that looked like a wolf.

"I would advise you not to make any abrupt moves. Beauty isn't a full-blood wolf, though she's close enough. The dog in her only seems to exacerbate her temperament."

Moving slowly, he faced the creature and knelt down, so they were at face level. Rolling on his back, he spread his arms. Beauty whimpered and took a cautious step toward him, finally licking his face. Raising his head, Buck kissed the wolf dog on its fanged muzzle.

"You got a set of balls on you," Esme said. "But I guess I already had that part figured out."

Buck grasped the large beast's neck and hugged it. Though the wolf dog wasn't wagging its tail, it was obvious she was already enamored by the big cowboy. Standing behind them and suddenly unable to resist the two wrestling on the floor.

"This gorgeous animal's name is Beauty?" Buck asked.

"You apparently have a sixth sense of which I wasn't aware," Esme said.

"She is a beauty," Buck said.

"If you can pull away from your frivolity, I

think we have a matter to discuss."

Buck quit scratching behind Beauty's ears and glanced up at Esme.

"I'm at your service," he said.

Esme grinned. "That's what I like hearing a man say. Let's take a dip in the hot tub and relax. There we can talk."

Kristy was gone, having slipped out of the teepee without saying goodbye. Buck followed Esme out the flap to a large wooden tub, barely illuminated by moon and starlight. Stripping naked, she climbed the stairs up to the deck surrounding the tub, dipped a cautious toe into the hot water, and then immersed herself up to her neck. Buck hesitated in taking off his clothes.

"Don't be bashful," Esme said. "You weren't last night, and I've already seen you naked."

Although fraught with feelings of impropriety, he removed his clothes and eased into the hot water, fingers of steam wafting up from its surface.

"Where is the heat coming from?"

"The tub is wood-fired. I have no electricity here."

"It's wonderful. I've never sat in a hot tub beneath the stars before."

"There is nothing else like it in the world."

His passions ignited by hot water and the proximity of Esme's naked body, Buck closed his eyes, luxuriating in the attention she was giving him. Beauty bayed at the hazy moon. When the plaintiff howl died away, he reached over the side of the hot tub and rubbed the big animal's head.

"I've never heard a howl that sounded quite like hers does," he said.

"As I told you, she is part wolf and part dog. When she sings to the moon, her voice is very distinctive and different from both. There's not another animal on earth that sounds like her."

"That's a fact. I'd recognize that howl from

miles away."

"And you'll never forget it," she said.

Buck finally relaxed, more comfortable when water had covered most of his body. Esme removed the cork from a jug of wine, tipped it over her shoulder, and drank a healthy slug. She handed the bottle to him.

"This isn't going to make me do strange things, is it?"

"Depends on how affected you are by cheap red wine," Esme said.

Buck tipped the bottle over his shoulder and drank as distant lightning flashed across the sky.

Esme laughed when he said, "This doesn't taste like Skeleton Creek Cabernet."

"Potent wine isn't always expensive. A spring storm approaches," she said. "Do you believe in spirits?"

"I saw a ghost once."

"Sure it was a ghost?"

"I was drunk. I still believe what I saw was the ghost of a girl who had died because of unexplained circumstances."

"I'm glad you have an open mind. Most would deny their own eyes."

"Why are you asking about ghosts?"

"You've elected to complete your duties as Fertility Deity. There are things you must know, and things I must know about you."

"I have no idea what you're talking about," Buck said. "Doesn't matter though because your wine and this hot water have me relaxed to the point that I'm tuned in on every word you say."

"You're smiling. I am serious."

"Sorry," Buck said. "Please ask me anything."

"I'm a full-blood Native American, in case you haven't noticed."

"There's isn't much I haven't noticed about you," he said.

"I belong to the Mississippian Tribe."

"Never heard of it."

"That's because there are no longer any Mississippians alive."

"Except for you?"

"Not even me," she said. "I'm from another time and place."

"You mean like an alien from outer space?"

"Stop grinning. I'm deadly serious, and I'm not an extraterrestrial."

"What are you, then?"

"A traveler through time. I live in the past; a thousand years ago in the eastern part of Oklahoma."

Buck's smile had disappeared. "I'm listening."

"I traveled from a distant time and place to instruct these women about my religion. Do you believe me?"

"I don't often sit in a hot tub drinking wine with a beautiful woman. Your story sounds a little crazy. Doesn't matter because I'd tell you anything you want to hear if it'll keep you beside me."

It was Esme's turn to smile. "At least you're honest. That's an important trait. You passed the first test."

"I didn't realize I was being graded," he said.

"Lana chose you. She picked well. I think you'll make a fine Fertility Deity."

"Maybe you better tell me the rest of my duties."

"If I told you, you'd refuse the remainder of your task."

Buck glanced at the cloudy darkness as heat lightning lighted the sky.

"How do you know that?" he asked.

"I am a medicine woman. I can read you like an open book. You don't have a deceitful bone in that gorgeous body of yours. You are also a thoughtful man. Your final task is best completed without too much forethought."

"At least give me a clue."

"You're the detective. You already have your clue."

"You make it sound so ominous," he said.

"Most men would have no problem completing the task. I sense you are different."

"Tell me," he said.

"What you are about to do will be part of you till the day you die, and will result in a profound change in your life."

"In a bad way?"

"You'll not be harmed or have to harm anyone. Profound changes aren't always bad or good. If you are afraid of change, then get dressed and go. The task can wait another year."

"I feel I've known you forever, and I trust you. I'll stay."

Esme handed him a brownie from the covered basket.

"Pot-laced," she said when Buck bit into the chewy treat. "But don't worry. There isn't enough there to do any damage."

Approaching storms continued moving toward them. The sky, at least for the moment was luminous, with glowing stars and a golden moon that was almost full. A familiar voice interrupted them.

"We want our share," someone said from the darkness.

It was Sara and Lana.

"We came for a soak and brought some good wine, not Esme's cheap swill."

Wine and pot were already working on Buck as Lana and Sara shed their clothes and joined them in the hot tub. Lana, the buttoned-down businessperson, had the looks of a movie star and body of a stripper. He had almost gotten used to being nude when she touched his thigh.

Esme extinguished the torches, the lack of ambient light affording them a perfect view of moon and stars, along with flickering fireflies lighting the clearing. The bold, red, native wine and pot-laced brownies had rendered him anesthetized.

An Oklahoma spring storm approached them, distant thunder sounding ever closer. A south breeze scattered fingers of steam rising off the hot water. The wind had intensified, along with rain dappling the hot tub's surface. He remembered following Esme, Sara, and Lana out of the water, and little else.

Chapter 14

Buck's psyche had descended into a dream world, some place other than here and now. Darkness cloaked him like a damp blanket. Still quite naked, he trod barefoot along a narrow trail surrounded by trees that blocked moon and starlight. Something lay ahead, waiting for him. He stopped, not wanting to proceed, though knew he had to.

His dream transmuted into a different time and place. He lay naked on a thick bearskin rug with Esme and Sara, stroking his shoulders with deft fingers, kneeling behind him. The flap of the teepee opened, and Lana entered, naked except for a cloak of colorful feathers draping her shoulders.

Flickering firelight illuminated the teepee, allowing Buck to perceive reality or at least his perception of it amid blurry shadows. Incense filled his nostrils with the odor of cloves, mingling with Lana's perfume and her woman-smell as she approached him.

She followed his eyes, long legs spread wide as Sara and Esme stood and removed her cloak of feathers. His eyes had become unfocused, fixated on the hair on her head and pubic region almost green in the eerie light of Esme's glimmering fire.

Slowly bending her long, dancer's legs, she straddled him.

Esme's fire disappeared, replaced by the darkness of a forest path. Sharp pebbles gouged his feet as he inched toward shadows beyond a bend. An unknown being, large and frightening, waited for him. It didn't matter. Something unexplainable continued to draw him toward the darkness.

Lana lay beneath him, her big green eyes rolling, along with her body moving to the crescendo of a mental orchestra. Esme and Sara kneeled beside them, chanting and laying on hands as Buck and Lana made passionate love in the teepee's muted light.

"Who are you?" Buck asked as he stared at the dark man in his path.

The man, or strange and powerful being he might be, didn't answer.

"Let me pass," Buck said, stepping forward until stopped by strong hands.

"Where is the man with the two blond women?" the dark man demanded.

Buck shook his head. "Let me pass."

With eyes glowing supernatural green, the wraith squeezed Buck's shoulders until they ached.

"Tell me."

"I have no idea what you're talking about."

"Yes, you do. Take me to the dog killer."

***

Buck awoke wrapped in a colorful Indian rug on the floor of Esme's teepee. Beauty had a mouthful of the rug, yanking it to get his attention. Patting her head, he rubbed behind her ears.

"Morning, big girl. Where's your mama?"

As if to show him, Beauty went to the door, gazed out and then returned. Buck grinned when he pulled off the blanket and realized he was quite naked. He had only the dimmest of memories of what had happened after leaving the hot tub. Something had happened, though he couldn't remember what it was. It didn't seem to matter because he felt wonderfully alive and stoked beyond imagination. Esme entered the tent as he was dressing.

"Have a good time last night?" she asked.

"Too good," he said. "I don't remember much after eating that brownie. I need to go home soon, so I'm ready to finish my duties."

"Your duties are complete. Kristy's on her way here to get you."

Buck rubbed his forehead. "Don't play games."

"No games. You really don't remember?"

"Just the nightmare that woke me up."

Kristy had opened the flap of the teepee before Buck and Esme had a chance to finish their conversation.

"You ready?" she asked.

Buck finished dressing and followed her out the tent flap. When they reached the clearing, she began pointing out landmarks.

"That building is our library," she said. "It has more books than they have at OU."

"I'm impressed. What about doctors?"

"We have a fully-staffed clinic with many of the amenities of a small hospital."

The police station was a partially aboveground building with a garage area for their strange vehicles. Banks of solar panels sat on the roof, apparently generating electricity to power them. He also noticed a windmill, its giant rotor turning slowly in an Oklahoma breeze.

"Is there anything you don't have here?"

Kristy grinned and said, "Men."

Chapter 15

Buck thanked Hector for performing his feeding duties and watching Pard. The young Mexican with a noticeable limp and prominent Spanish accent simply shrugged and smiled.

"Hey, no problem. You help me out plenty. Me and LaDona love Pard."

"He's a great dog. I got you something for your trouble." Buck gave him a bottle of Jack Daniel's. He grinned when Buck added, "I know you like tequila better, but I got you, Black Jack, instead."

Hector, Buck knew, didn't like tequila and it was a mark of their friendship they could joke about ethnic stereotypes. Lady whinnied and shook her head to show her pleasure when he finally reached her stall.

"How's my Lady?" he asked, stroking her regal neck before giving her a mighty hug.

Lady was happier to see him than annoyed by his disregard. She was also eager for a run. Buck didn't disappoint, saddling and leading her out of the barn. They spent the better part of the morning galloping along a riding trail, Pard matching them stride for stride.

Pard raced between his feet as he washed and groomed Lady before returning the beautiful horse to her stall. It was only then that he thought about what he needed to do to proceed with the investigation. Pulling out the topo map Sheriff Hagen had given him, he located Clayton's ranch with his fingertip. Skeleton Creek lay just north of the house, and he traced the course he and Clayton had taken in the Jeep to view the dead cow.

An oil well pumped Oklahoma crude slowly from the ground at a nearby oil lease. The lease, like the dead cow, lay just north of Skeleton Creek and connected to a section line road. A notation on the road indicated the little town of Crescent was ten miles further north.

Not far, at least as the crow flies, from the spot where Clayton had found the dead cow, was Lykaia, entered from a lease road which ran east off the very same section line road that continued on to Crescent. Buck wanted to check things on the ground and considered loading Lady into his horse trailer and taking her with him to Clayton's.

"You better stay and watch out for Hector, LaDona and the baby," he said, rubbing Pard's ears.

Buck also left Lady at Sunset Farms, knowing Clayton had plenty of horses. By now, his hands knew Buck was working for him and didn't detain him at the front gate. It was already late afternoon, and he found Clayton strolling alone along a path in his Japanese garden.

"What's up?" he asked.

"I want to check out a few things on the north end of your ranch. Got a map and horse I can borrow?"

"You know I have a hundred horses. I got something even better." Clayton took his cell phone from his shirt pocket. "Garth, bring me a ranch map. I'm headed to the motor pool."

Buck followed him down the winding path, suddenly aware many of the plants had started to bloom, Clayton's garden ablaze with the colors and odors of early spring. They exited the garden through a rustic gate. Another path led to a large metal building. Clayton pointed a device at the overhead door, an electric engine slowly raising it to reveal a dozen or more four-wheelers.

"I never got on one of these contraptions myself. The boys use them to check the fences and outlying pastures. They get more work done now and in less time. Take one."

Familiar with the vehicles, Buck had ridden one once with friends. They were all the same, even painted with Clayton's ranch colors of orange and black. He picked the one closest to the front door, straddled it, and turned the key as Clayton's supervisor joined them.

"This is Garth Dunlap."

Buck shook the man's hand, realizing he was the younger brother of Roy Dunlap. He noticed the resemblance. Missing was Roy's buttoned-down image, replaced by the weathered skin of a man who had spent much of his life outdoors. Another man with a distinctive baby face joined them, handing Garth a map.

"I made a copy like you said. Need anything else?"

"No, Johnny, that'll do it."

The man cast a quizzical glance at Buck before returning the way he came.

"Just follow this road. It'll take you to the north pastures," Garth said.

Handing Buck the map, he followed the cowpoke named Johnny.

Buck watched him disappear around the corner and then asked, "Was that Johnny Crabtree?"

"Yep. Not much of a hand if you ask me. Garth likes him."

"You're not worried about him trying to sell one of your cows?"

Clayton smiled and shook his head. "That's why I hired you, Mr. Detective. Don't prove me wrong."

Cranking the four-wheeler, Buck headed up the path. Once out of sight, he stopped and examined the map Garth Dunlap had given him, apparently a copy Johnny Crabtree had made from an original. The handwritten words, Garth's map, occupied the upper left-hand corner. He also noticed several markings and notations, one of them on the fence line of the very pasture where he had assisted in investigating the murdered man. A good place to start, he decided.

All the gates had numerous locks, linked, so anyone who regularly used the gates had a key, or combination, to his own lock. Garth's map provided combinations for his locks and Buck had no trouble navigating the maze of gates and pathways to Clayton's northernmost fence.

The ATV had lots of muscle, enough to power a two-hundred-pound man down the road at more than fifty miles per hour. Still, early spring, a slight breeze, and the nip in the air made him glad he had worn his sleeveless down parka. He followed the fence line until he reached the penciled x Clayton's supervisor had made. Finding the general location, he began walking the fence; looking for some reason why Garth had marked it. He soon found what he was looking for.

To the unsuspecting eye, the section of fence was no different from the rest of the barrier. Closer inspection revealed something else entirely. Someone had rigged the fence so it would swing open with little effort. Without knowledge of the secret gate's location, it looked normal. The marking on the map made Garth a prime suspect in the rustling of Clayton's cows. After another glance at his topo map, he stared at the tree line marking the course of Skeleton Creek.

Buck headed north through the hidden gate in Clayton's fence. When he reached the tree line, he turned westward, searching for a trail leading down to the creek. He soon found the spot he was looking for. Once through the narrow breach, he slid the ATV down the steep bank. The big tires of the sure-footed vehicle would have made a potentially treacherous descent to the creek easy. It didn't matter because someone had modified the steep bank, lessening the angle down to the water. Someone also likely involved in the cattle theft.

A spring storm was brewing in the west, a wall cloud darkening the sky. Buck hadn't checked the weather report before leaving Sunset Farms and had no idea how severe the storm might be. If you lived in Oklahoma long enough, you knew the weather was always subject to abrupt change.

Tracks of both horses and cattle marked the mud and dirt around the creek bed. He had no trouble tracking them as they turned in a westerly direction. Overhanging limbs of trees on both sides of the creek formed a roof-like enclosure, resulting in a darkened tunnel. The approaching storm made the path even darker, causing him to switch on the vehicle's lone headlamp.

Buck didn't bother stopping to check the topo map because he felt sure the path of the cattle headed toward the oil lease located just north of Skeleton Creek. Hundreds of creeks, some large and some small, dissect central Oklahoma. Many of them remain almost dry during much of the year though carry lots of water during the spring and fall rainy seasons. Skeleton Creek was no different. Larger than most and always carrying some water, it often became a roaring torrent during periods of heavy rainfall.

Buck soon found the spot where the rustlers had driven the cattle out of the creek bed. Again, he had no trouble powering the ATV up the slope. The first thing he saw upon exiting the tree line was a single pumping unit, its polished rod screeching as it moved slowly up and down.

The sky had darkened noticeably, a fine mist of rain beginning to fall. A lease fence encircled the pumping unit. Oil leases are dangerous places and pump jacks heavy pieces of constantly moving machinery. Because of this, Oklahoma law requires oil operators to maintain a security fence around them and to keep them locked.

Buck soon solved the puzzle. Prompted by his discovery at Clayton's ranch, he scanned the back of the fence for just such an entry, his search soon rewarded. Pulling back a hidden gate, he entered the lease with ease.

Most oil leases are usually bare dirt paved with just enough gravel to allow access to large trucks. The sky was growing darker by the minute, but Buck could easily see hoof prints of horses, and the cattle someone had herded there from Clayton's ranch. Whoever had used the oil lease to load the stolen cattle was also someone who had access to the well. The sign fronting the oil tanks pegged Crescent Oil Company as the owner. Buck wasn't surprised.

The map unwittingly provided by Garth Dunlap, implicated him in the rustling. His brother Roy, the president of Crescent Oil, had access to the lease and could easily have supplied a key or combination to get the cattle trailer in and out of the front gate. Buck had little time to ponder Garth and Roy's complicity in the theft as rain continued falling, lightly at first and then in a pelting torrent. Resetting the fence, he straddled the ATV and started back toward Clayton's ranch.

Oklahoma red clay provides firm footing during dry weather. When rain begins, it becomes treacherously slick. Buck realized as much as he tracked his path back to Skeleton Creek. The formerly gentle flow had reverted to a swirling torrent of rushing water, probably exasperated by flooding upstream.

ATVs are sure-footed vehicles. Still, when he pointed the front wheels down the slope, he realized he had made a mistake. The front end slipped sideways, out of control, and then flipped over, dumping him into the slick mud. The work someone had done to lessen the slope down to the creek had also compromised its integrity. Water poured down the opening, washing away any traction that may have existed. For Buck, it didn't matter as he tumbled toward moving water, the ATV rolling on top of him.

The weight of the little vehicle carried him into the torrent Skeleton Creek had suddenly become, and rushing water propelled him rapidly downstream. He had swallowed lots of water, and his muscles felt like warm putty when he finally grabbed a log lodged against the bank and pulled himself up the slippery slope, somewhat out of the water.

Rain continued to fall, but the brunt of the rapidly moving storm had already passed over. He lay in the mud for a while, spitting up water and trying to catch his breath. When his strength finally returned, he found he had another problem.

Mud was so slick it sucked one of his boots right off of his foot. When he tried to stand, his feet came out from under him, and he plunged back into the muck. Finally reaching the relative stability of a red sandstone boulder, he stretched out on his back and drew an exhausted breath.

As he rested on the rock, the storm abated, replaced by darkness. It made the creek bed seem almost like the inside of a cave. Using roots and stone, he finally managed to work himself above the rushing water. What he found was a game trail, established by decades, maybe even centuries, of wild animals.

Supported by rock and roots, the narrow pathway provided his first sure footing since exiting the oil lease. He was drenched, his cap gone, along with one of his favorite boots, and he had to pick his way on the trail because it was too dark to see. He also had the uneasy feeling something was tracking him.

Chapter 16

Buck continued along the narrow game trail, apprehensive he might lose his footing and tumble back into the raging water. He had no other option as very little light filtered through the roof of interlocking branches. Something in the distance, an animal coughing to let creatures in the forest know it was on the prowl, also raised his anxiety level. The eerie sound caused a sudden increase in his heart rate. Even though he had never heard it before, he knew it was Clayton's panther.

Whumph! A throaty cough echoed down the narrow valley formed by Skeleton Creek. The beast was close. Because of the darkness and resonance of sound, he couldn't tell just how close. Groping for a branch or rock to use as a weapon, he found nothing.

Subdued rain continued to fall. The sound of gusting wind was at times almost deafening, instantly lowering the pressure in the arboreal tunnel whenever a blow began. Lacking vision, his hearing, and sense of smell compensated. He could almost taste the loamy odor of thick mud coating his body. He also sensed another storm was approaching.

Having lost track of time, he knew Clayton would soon miss him, and send out a search party. With this in mind, he yelled "Hello." Nothing but the roar of gusting wind answered him.

Muscles aching from exhaustion, he wanted only to hunker down and wait until morning. The cough of the panther caused him to decide differently. He continued picking his way along the slope until a scream behind him chilled his soul. Turning, he faced the monster he couldn't see that was close enough for him to smell.

He had heard panthers make a noise like the scream of a woman. Now he knew it was true. He also realized the panther wanted him to make his presence known, and he could only imagine the beast in a crouch, fangs bared, ready to spring and tear him to shreds. Within seconds, his nightmare became all too real.

The weight of the heavy cat hammered him into the mud. Jaws would have clamped his jugular, holding him in place with two large paws until his last breath escaped from his body. Buck had ducked and pivoted, the beast's claws raking only his back. Having no other weapon, he grabbed a double handful of mud, thrusting it into the panther's eyes.

Some primeval instinct guided his hands, the panther howling in outrage when struck in the face with the globs of sticky mud. The ruse worked for only a moment, though long enough for him to dive down the ledge to the creek.

The fall should have knocked him silly, except he landed in shallow water. Plowing ahead, his heart beating fast as his mind raced for answers, knowing the panther would be on him in a flash. The water wasn't deep, though was flowing rapidly, and he let the current carry him forward. Though he couldn't hear the big cat, he somehow knew it was bounding after him. When he reached solid ground, he sprang to his feet and began running toward the light, maybe from the moon, on the roof of the arboreal tunnel. He didn't make it very far.

Tripping on a pile of brush, he slid to a painful halt in fine sand and gravel. Turning, he saw the panther for the first time. Like a monster, its eyes glowed red in muted moonlight, muscles rippling in its powerful frame. The big cat was solid black.

Scooping a handful of gravel, he tossed it at the beast, his efforts doing nothing to slow the cat's movement toward him. Having no other weapon, he threw another handful of gravel and then waited for the cat to lunge, unable to move because of a twisted ankle.

Hearing a mortal growl directly behind him, he turned to see Beauty, Esme's giant wolf dog. Stepping in front of him, she braced for the cat's attack. Beauty was big, though not nearly as big as the panther. Still, she crouched with lowered head and bared fangs, dancing from side to side, daring the cat to attack her. He soon did, missing her neck as he rolled her in the creek bottom.

Beauty didn't miss his but failed to catch the jugular. She had the big cat by the back of its neck, painful but not lethal. The panther turned on its back, bucking and flailing its claws, trying to shake the powerful animal off its neck. Buck continued groping in the semi-darkness, finally finding a heavy piece of driftwood. Hoping not to strike Beauty, he dived on the two beasts, nailing the big cat between the eyes, and then continuing to swing.

The panther could have taken either Buck or Beauty alone, though not both. Managing to clip her head with one large paw, it backed away, snarling, and then disappeared into the darkness. Buck lay exhausted, his arms around the huge wolf dog. Beauty was on the ground, her muscles twitching and breath coming in labored gasps. His hands were sticky with the ooze of warm blood—his, Beauty's, the panther's, or maybe all three. Tearing off what remained of his shirt he stuffed it into the gaping wound in the big wolf dog's side and applied pressure.

~•~

Buck had lost all concept of time when someone shook his shoulder. He stared up into Esme's mystical eyes. Stuffing something into his mouth, she told him to swallow it.

"You are hurt, though not as badly as Beauty. I gave you something for the pain. Now you need to help me with her."

"How did you find us?"

Her smile flashed in muted moonlight. "Our thoughts are connected in a subconscious collective. You called for help, and I came."

Her explanation made him grin. Whatever drug she had given him had already begun working. Releasing his grip on the big wolf dog, he raised himself into a sitting position. Esme began working on Beauty. The big cat had raked bloody claw marks across her right side. After removing what was left of Buck's shirt from the wound, she dabbed it with a medicine-coated rag and then bound it tightly with a large bandage. Slipping a pill into Beauty's mouth, she massaged the animal's throat until she swallowed it.

"The pill is more than medicine and will give both of you a physical boost. I'll lead us out of here. You'll need to help her along."

When Beauty rose up on her haunches, Buck hugged her, though careful not to do further damage.

"You saved my life," he said, kissing her right on the mouth.

They spent the next hour slowly hiking to Esme's teepee. The storm had blown over leaving only wispy clouds that now barely cloaked

110

twinkling stars and hazy moon. Crickets and tree frogs had begun singing, and they could still hear the panther in the distance. When they reached her encampment, Esme took them inside and handed him a ladle of water.

"Wait while I cleanse Beauty's wounds. She's in much worse shape than you are."

Buck sipped water laced with medicine Esme thought would help him and waited as she worked on the big animal.

"Will she make it?" he asked when she finally returned to check on him.

"The cat injured her, and she has lost lots of blood. She would have died if you hadn't staunched the flow with your shirt."

"I'll feel horrible if she doesn't pull through."

Esme smiled. "She'll make it. She has a big heart. I stitched her wounds and gave her medicine and herbs to start the healing process."

"You're a wonder woman."

"Now it's your turn. Come outside and let's get the rest of your clothes off."

Buck had no clue how stiff his muscles had become until he tried to stand. A big woman, Esme pulled him to his feet and then helped him outside to a makeshift shower. She stripped away what remained of his muddy clothes, and he stood naked beneath a canvas water bag as she bathed him with a sponge.

"You need stitches in your shoulder," she said when she finished washing away the last of the caked blood and mud. "The cat really nailed you. I'm surprised you got away from it."

"No one more surprised than me. I was about ready to kiss my ass goodbye when Beauty showed up."

"I doubt it, Buck McDivit. You don't have an ounce of quit in your body."

Esme kissed him, gave him another painkiller,

and then sewed up the wound on his shoulder. After administering a healing balm, she bandaged it securely.

"Now," she said. "I have one last potion for you."

Esme gave him a goblet filled with a semi-sweet liquid he could not identify.

"What is it?"

"An aphrodisiac. No way am I taking a gorgeous hunk of man to bed with me unless he can perform."

Although stiff and sore, Buck awoke in surprisingly good spirits, feeling lucky to be alive. Beauty was awake. When he raised his head, she licked his face and demanded a hug.

"You saved my life big girl. You look as stiff and sore as I am."

The blankets were warm. He'd never known sleeping on the ground could be so comfortable. Quite naked, he was looking around for something to wear when Kristy appeared through the flap.

"Don't worry, Cowboy. We won't make you walk around exposed all day, though I wouldn't mind." She handed him shirt and jeans, both new. "Esme threw away your filthy clothes."

"Just my size. How'd you manage?"

"Don't get the big head. We have several stores in Lykaia. I know about how tall you are, and we used your belt to determine your waist size."

Kristy handed him his belt, and he worked it through the jean loops. He was tucking in his shirt when Esme entered the teepee.

"You look good. My therapy must have helped."

"Best I ever had. In fact, I could use a little more."

Esme put a hand up. "You have other things to do right now."

"Great, I don't even have my boots."

"You'll have to wear moccasins. I sent out a patrol to Skeleton Creek this morning. They found your wallet and cell phone but not your other boot."

When Kristy stepped outside, he glanced at the missed messages on his phone.

"Better call Clayton. I'm sure he's wondering what happened to me."

"Don't tell him about the panther."

Though Buck started to say something, he thought better of it. Clayton answered on the first ring.

"Where the hell are you? I had the boys out all night. They found the ATV and one of your boots. I thought you were dead."

"A little mishap. I misplaced my phone, or I'd have called sooner."

"Where are you now?"

"Lykaia. Can you send someone to get me?"

"Sheriff Hagen's already on the way. I'll give him a call."

"Still have a job?" Esme asked when he put the phone in his pocket.

"Clayton's too much of a control freak to fire me before wringing out every last drop of information. Why didn't you want me to tell him about the panther?"

"I can't explain just yet. Please just trust me for now."

Kristy reentered the teepee before he could question Esme further. "It was Lana. The sheriff is here and wants to see you."

"That was fast," Buck said.

<hr>

One of the Lykaia vehicles waited for them outside the teepee. Buck and Kristy climbed into the back. The two compound cops drove them to the front of the Lykaia general headquarters where they found Lana and Sheriff Hagen. He cast a disbelieving glance at Buck's moccasins and motioned him to get in his squad car.

"Want to tell me what happened last night?" he said as they drove out the front gate.

Buck shook his head. "I'm not sure I know myself."

"Uh huh."

He knew the young cowboy well enough to realize he probably had a good reason for his silence. It didn't stop him from asking.

Pressed for details, Buck said, "I'm on to something. I don't have a firm handle just yet."

"At least give me a hint."

Buck told him about the oil lease, withholding what he now knew about Garth and Roy Dunlap, and glossing over, in deference to Esme, the panther attack. Sheriff Hagen didn't miss a word.

"What have you got going with the people in the commune?"

"I told you. They asked me to help them catch the intruder, and I'm doing it, with Clayton's blessing."

"I don't mind you working both sides of the fence. Just don't try it with me."

"You have my word."

"At least let me provide a little backup."

Sheriff Hagen grinned and shook his head when Buck said, "Not just yet. If I get in a bind, you'll be the first person I call."

Chapter 17

Sheriff Hagen dropped Buck off at the front gate of Clayton's ranch. Two cowhands escorted him, still carrying his lone boot under his arm, to the veranda. Clayton wasn't alone, KK standing behind him, massaging his shoulders. Buck did a double take when he saw her skimpy babydoll nightie, the transparent garment doing little to cloak her marvelous body. She smiled when she saw him, hurried over, and gave him a wiggly hug.

"We've been so worried about you."

Buck glanced at Clayton and instantly knew KK was using him to elicit a little jealousy from her rich lover. By his pained expression, he realized she had scored a direct hit. She let go of him when Clayton tossed him his other boot.

"Now tell me just where the hell you've been."

Buck glanced at KK, her cagey grin reminding him of the very reason they had broken up. She was a tease, and he finally grew weary of her playing him like a fiddle, sometimes second fiddle. He wrestled on his boots as Clayton waited for an explanation.

After telling a doctored version of what had happened, he saw little reason to hamper his investigation by ratting out supervisor Garth and business partner Roy Dunlap. It didn't matter because his abbreviated story seemed to satisfy Clayton. He rang for Maria to bring him a refill on his whiskey. Buck could see when she brought it KK's skimpy attire appalled her. Clayton didn't seem to notice.

"I'm leaving for Kansas City in a few days. Roy and me are going to a cattle auction."

And probably a dozen topless joints, Buck thought. When he glanced at KK, she smiled and winked at him, probably thinking the same thing.

Clayton walked him to his Navigator. "How close are you to getting me some answers?"

"Don't shoot me, Boss. I'm working fast as I can."

"I know," Clayton said, giving Buck's shoulder a fatherly tap "What am I going to do with KK?"

"I don't have a clue what you're talking about."

"Yes, you do. You saw her, parading around half-naked. The hands are all talking behind my back and Maria will hardly look me in the eye."

"KK's a lot of woman. You knew it when you took up with her."

"You think she's too much woman for me?"

Buck grinned. "I don't know about you. She was more than a handful for me. I finally had to call calf rope."

Clayton smiled as Buck cranked the Navigator's engine. He nodded and started to put the vehicle into gear. Clayton raised a hand to stop him.

"Yes, sir?"

"I'd like to take the lady at the commune up on her offer to visit the place."

"When would you like to go?"

Clayton glanced at his Rolex. "How about right now?"

"Why the hell not?" Buck said, dialing Lana.

"When would he like to come?" she asked

upon answering.

"Right now."

"Not much notice."

"Mr. O'Meara is a man of action."

"Bring him over. I'll personally escort him."

Clayton listened to the one-sided conversation, smiling when Buck nodded.

"We're on. How long will it take you to get ready?"

"I was born ready," he said with a wolfish grin. "Let me get my hat."

Like Buck and almost every other cowboy on the ranch, Clayton usually wore a Stetson. They both looked sharp in their pressed Levi's and Western-cut shirts, and Buck felt better wearing his favorite boots again instead of the moccasins. Clayton's big silver belt buckle bore the shape of a rodeo bull and accented a slender waistline for a man his age.

"Which vehicle?" Buck asked.

"You drive. I'm just along for the ride. How far is it?"

"As the crow flies, the compound is beyond Skeleton Creek, just over the hill. Since we don't have wings, it's a little more round-about getting there."

"I'm not going to have any surprises, am I?"

Buck grinned. "Surprises, hell, I'm not sure you'll believe your eyes."

"Now you've piqued my interest."

"I won't spoil it for you. You'll see for yourself soon enough."

The two familiar female guards met them at the front gate, escorting them in their electric vehicle to the main business area. Clayton drank in the windmills and half-buried structures they drove past. The two women let them out at the front door of the administration building.

"Lana is expecting you."

"Thanks," Buck said as he and Clayton climbed out of the vehicle.

Clayton followed Buck down the short flight of stairs and past the young woman sitting at the control desk that simply smiled and waved them toward Lana's office. Clayton apparently expected a stodgy old woman instead of a beautiful red haired beauty with eyes a color of green that few humans have. When she turned and smiled, he yanked off his hat, slicked his silver hair and mustache with a quick swipe of his big hand, and then returned her smile with one of his own.

"I am Lana, Chief Administrator of Lykaia. You must be Mr. O'Meara."

"Clayton, call me Clayton," he said, taking her hand and holding it a bit too long.

Clayton was tall and unused to looking into the eyes of a woman fully six-feet tall herself.

"I'm sorry we haven't met before now," she said.

"If I had known such a gorgeous woman was running the place, I would have stopped by long ago."

Lana didn't blush at Clayton's blatant come-on. Having known her effect on men for many years, as Buck saw it, anything less would likely have disappointed her. Instead, she shot back with a compliment of her own.

"If I had known what a good-looking man owned the ranch next to us, I would have visited you first."

"I like you," he said. "You have a certain quality I can't quite describe."

They both laughed when she said, "Balls?"

"Buck told me a little about this place. I'm curious to have a look around."

"This place is Lykaia. It's probably quite different from anywhere else you have ever visited, and I don't think you'll be disappointed."

Clayton grabbed her hand again. "After meeting you, nothing else I see will disappoint me. I am already enchanted."

"Clayton, you are full of it," she said with a smile, pulling her hand away from his grasp and giving him a playful slap across the cheek.

Buck watched in amazement, thinking they might rip off each other's clothes any minute and go at it on the floor. They refrained themselves, but both smiled as they left the office and walked upstairs. Kristy was waiting for them, and her own smile turned to a pout when she touched the long scratch on Buck's face and neck. Lana and Clayton didn't notice as she led him to an electric vehicle with no top or sides.

"Sit in back with me," Lana said. "Kristy will drive. Buck can sit up front with her."

Clayton climbed in, not missing Lana's show of abundant long legs as she hiked her already short skirt to step up into the vehicle.

"It will be my pleasure," he said,

There are no mountains in Logan County, though it isn't flat. Changes in elevation of a hundred feet or more are common. Buck got his own first look at some of the area as they drove away from the administration buildings.

"Much of Lykaia is below ground. We have an extensive complex of tunnels that join offices, private residences, restaurants, and recreational facilities. We generate the energy it takes to run our community using wind, solar, or other green means. We have a sophisticated grid unduplicated any place on earth."

"Interesting," Clayton said. "What do you do when the wind isn't blowing?"

"I detect skepticism in your voice."

"I'm in the oil business. I know of no other way to produce all the energy the world needs except by the use of fossil fuels."

"Then maybe you should open your eyes and learn a few things. Enough wind exists to supply all the energy the world will ever need. You just have to know how to harness it."

"But at what price?" he asked.

"Can you put a price on the quality of life?"

"No one wants to live without heat in the winter and air conditioning in the summer, especially here in Oklahoma."

"We have heat and air, and even indoor plumbing. One thing is different; we don't pollute. Look around," Lana said, pointing from one side of the vehicle to the other. "We have created a virtual Eden here."

Clayton grinned. "There must be a snake around someplace."

Crossing her arms tightly and pointing her knees away from him, she said, "I'm not talking to you anymore."

"Oh, come on now. I was only pulling your leg." Lana had to smile and shake her head when he added, "At least I'd like to pull your leg."

Lana and Clayton continued to banter like love-struck teens as Kristy drove them around Lykaia. They passed an outdoor swimming pool landscaped and designed to emulate a South Pacific lagoon. Clayton grew silent and his eyes larger when he noticed many of the female swimmers and loungers were either nude or at least partially so.

"We also have indoor and outdoor tennis courts and a nine-hole golf course. Do you golf?"

"Some of my friends consider me pretty damn good."

"Fine because I don't like playing people I can easily trounce."

"I wouldn't want to take advantage of you. Although you don't know it, I had a golf scholarship at Oklahoma State."

"So did I. Mine was at OU."

It was Clayton's turn to fold his arms. "I might have known. I've never met anyone from OU yet who didn't think they could beat anyone at anything."

"You find something wrong with that?"

"No, and I'm going to love whipping your gorgeous ass in golf."

"You're on, big boy. Care to put a little money where your mouth is?"

"You bet I do. I've never had a woman beat me at golf, much less a Sooner."

"Well I've never had a man beat me at golf, especially an Aggie," she said, using a nickname for Oklahoma State students and graduates.

Kristy stopped the electric vehicle at the top of a hill overlooking the projecting roof of an underground building. A huge satellite dish sat mounted on the roof, along with a large telescope.

"This is our science laboratory. High-speed computers connect us with similar facilities around the world. We even exchange information with NASA."

"I haven't seen any livestock," Clayton said.

"We raise catfish in underground ponds and are big into hydroponics. We grow fruit and vegetables year round and trade for what meat and dairy products we consume."

"I'll admit your landscaping impresses me, as do your buildings. Who is your architect?"

"All our work is done in-house. We have scientists, artists, musicians, and excellent chefs living here. Lykaia encourages creativity and basks in the wealth created by our highly intelligent populace."

Clayton stared in awe. "Who supports this place?"

"We trade stocks and commodities on the world market and have our fingers in lots of financial pies. We run our own bank and lend money to women all over the world."

Kristy drove past the row of windmills and Lykaia's solar generation plant, neither Lana nor Clayton missing a beat in the back seat.

"You said you have indoor plumbing. Do you use septic tanks?"

"Hardly. We have a sewage reclamation plant that returns most of the water back to the earth in pristine form. We use the solid waste for energy generation, compost, and fertilizer. An improvement we devised on a technique developed by NASA for use on the space station."

"Impressive."

They soon reached the edge of Lykaia's property on a hill looking south. Kristy stopped the vehicle, pointing out Clayton's ranch in the distance. The setting sun cast a warm glow on brown buildings with roofs the color of teal that evoked the look of distant gemstones.

"There is much more to see underground. Still interested?"

"Wouldn't miss it for the world," Clayton said. "Lead the way. I'm a willing follower."

Chapter 18

Kristy turned the vehicle around though not in the direction from where they had come. Instead, she followed the rustic wooden fence line around the perimeter. They passed the pond where Buck and the others had taken a dip following the night of revelry. They also passed the thick stand of trees familiar to Buck because of the location of Esme's teepee. A woman in uniform met them at the door of the administration building and drove away in the vehicle.

Kristy and Buck lagged behind as Clayton followed Lana down the long tunnel. Squeezing his hand, she kissed his cheek. Clayton and Lana didn't notice, too intent on each other and the cool lights illuminating the tunnel. Lana commented about the lighting before Clayton had a chance to ask.

"It's like the illumination created by light-emitting diodes. It uses very little energy and results in almost no heat loss. It is lighting at its most efficient."

"Interesting, and the temperature seems perfect. How do you maintain it at such a constant level?"

"We have a central control point which

monitors temperature and energy usage in every building."

When they reached the Tiers Restaurant, a smiling hostess escorted them to Lana's table.

"I'll have a double martini," she said. "Clayton?"

"Thought you'd never ask. Jack Daniel's, neat, and make it a double."

The usual string quartet played in the background, accompanied by a woman with a wonderful voice singing an Italian aria. Clayton seemed enthralled as he downed his whiskey and motioned a passing waitress for another.

"The acoustics are marvelous, and the aroma coming from the kitchen makes me remember I missed lunch."

"You won't miss dinner. We have no menu here. We'll feast on the meal of the evening, and I promise you won't be disappointed."

"I've yet to be disappointed by anything," he said, his voice becoming mellow as he sipped his whiskey. She grinned, not answering when he added, "What else do you promise?"

Kristy and Buck held hands under the table, listening to Clayton and Lana's conversation as they ate their Santa Fe-style salmon enchiladas. Clayton was still smiling when they finished and moved to a dark bar offsetting the dining area. They had the secluded spot all alone, except for the friendly bartender who seemed to know Lana's importance and treated her accordingly. Lana's significant other soon joined them.

"I'm Sara," the small blond woman said, shaking Clayton's hand.

"Charmed," he said.

Feeling the effect of Lykaia's whiskey, he kissed her hand, unsure or not caring what her appearance meant. Sara seemed to sense that Clayton was an important guest. Buck and Kristy moved down a stool to allow her to sit beside Lana. Clayton and Lana's lively conversation continued, joined now by Sara's succinct comments and wry sense of humor. None of them noticed when Kristy and Buck moved to a dark booth.

"You okay?" she asked, again caressing the claw mark on Buck's face.

"Beauty took the brunt of the panther's attack. She's the one we should worry about."

"She's up and walking. Esme says she'll be good as new in a week or so. Can we sneak out of here?"

It was Buck's turn to smile. "With my two bosses getting snockered together at the bar, I don't think so."

"The way they are arguing, you would think they are an old married couple."

"Except both of them are smiling and Clayton has his hand on Lana's knee. I hope Sara doesn't cold cock him."

"She likes it. Clayton is getting Lana hot, and Sara knows she will be the recipient of her heat, later on, tonight."

"I'm getting hot talking about it."

Kristy squeezed his hand. "Then let's get out of here, and I'll take you to Esme's."

"I'll see what I can do," he said, returning to the bar. "You ready?"

Clayton glanced at Buck, shaking his head. "It's still early."

"Way past ten. We've been here all day and most of the night already."

"Lana and I will see he gets home," Sara said.

Buck glanced at Clayton for his acknowledgment. The nod he got spoke volumes. He returned to the booth where Kristy waited.

"Well?"

Buck grabbed her hand again and helped her to her feet, leading her back to the LED-lighted

hallway.
     "I think someone along with Sara is going to feel Lana's heat tonight."

Chapter 19

Buck reflected on his time with KK as he stopped by Sunset Farms the next morning to thank Hector once again for covering for him. Relationships come and go, and after time had passed following a break-up, he had a way of remembering the good things and forgetting the reasons for the split.

Seeing KK half-dressed on Clayton's veranda reminded him of the primary reason they had finally parted company. She had the body of a runway model and the face of a movie star. The trouble was, she knew it and played her advantage to the hilt.

Buck had all but forgotten the fights and arguments he'd had while dating her. Once, an angry cowboy had approached him on the dance floor of one of their favorite clubs. Without Buck knowing, the man had been buying drinks for KK all night. He intended to take her home with him, even if he had to fight Buck to do it.

Security guards, friends of his, had kicked the man out of the club, remedying the problem for him. KK acted the innocent angel, and he didn't learn until a few days later the reason for the altercation. Similar incidents had often occurred during the short time they'd dated.

On the way to Crescent Oil, he called Trey.

"How about lunch?"

"You buying?"

"Don't I always?"

"Then let's make it Nick's. They have the best jalapeno burgers in town."

"You got it," Buck said. "See you in an hour."

Sandy flashed him a pretty grin when he entered the ornate front doors of Crescent Oil.

"Hey, Cowboy, we missed you around here. Where you been?"

"Out of town. I'm back now. Seen Georgia?"

"Off for the day, running errands for Roy. She'll be at Nick's tonight."

"How do you know?"

"Because Roy's in Kansas City with Clayton and Georgia always starts her night at Nick's when he's out of town."

"Then maybe I'll see you both there later on."

Sandy blew him a kiss as he headed down the hall to his office. He liked their sexually charged teasing and knew Sandy also did, even if there was meager chance any meaningful relationship would ever come of it.

Buck checked his inbox and laptop for messages and email. No one except Sandy had seen him arrive. Finishing what he needed to do, he headed downstairs to Nick's. Trey had beaten him there and already taken a table in a darkened corner.

"What's up, Cowboy?" he asked as Buck grabbed a chair.

Buck told him about Lykaia, omitting details of the revel and his nights with Esme. He also told him about his adventure on the ATV. When he finished his story, he spread the crumpled topo map on the table in front of them, cocking a lamp to provide a little light in the dim restaurant.

"The reason we found Clayton's dead cow on the north side of Skeleton Creek is that the rustlers herded it there. It somehow got cut loose from the others, was tracked down and killed by the panther."

"That cat is a man-eater. We need to get some hunters out there and kill it."

"I promised Esme I wouldn't do that."

Trey looked straight into his eyes. "You know something, don't you?"

"The rustling and murder happened almost simultaneously. Garth Dunlap's map marked the likely spot where the rustler's got Clayton's cows out of the fence."

"Roy Dunlap's brother?"

Buck nodded. "My guess is he was involved in the rustling, along with Johnny Crabtree."

"Like I said before, there were probably three rustlers since Crabtree sold three cows at the auction, one cow for each of them. They stole the cattle for someone else but cut out three to sell for themselves and split the money. Sort of like a little extra bonus."

"And one of the cows they sold was Clayton's new breed."

"That's right," Trey said. "Most of the cows they rustled were probably the special ones. I think they intentionally took three regular cows to sell for their own account."

"And one of those got taken by the panther."

"So they had to sell one of the special cows," Trey said.

"They herded them north from Clayton's ranch, then down into Skeleton Creek," he said, pointing to a spot on the topo map. "They parked their cattle trailer at the oil lease, a lease owned by Crescent Oil. This implicates Roy Dunlap, or at least someone else who had access to entry into the well. Maybe they trucked the cattle up this lease-line road to the little settlement you told me about north of Crescent."

"If so, they probably have a holding pen around somewhere."

"My thoughts exactly," Buck said.

They ate their fries and jalapeno burgers, letting the fruit of their brainstorm session ferment a bit.

"I'm going to drive up and check it out," Trey finally said.

"Whoa, partner, not without me you're not."

Trey glanced at his watch. "Okay. What's wrong with right now?"

"That'll work. Let's take our vehicles to Sunset Farms. I have an old van I use for surveillance that's less suspicious than my Navigator or your red Wrangler.

Buck's faded brown van was more than thirty years old, its odometer long since broken. It didn't matter because he only used it occasionally. Happy to see them, Pard bounded into the van, jumped into Buck's lap and licked his face.

"Bring him," Trey said. "He's probably a better detective than either of us."

Buck didn't argue. Illegal tinting darkened the windows, and it seemed the perfect vehicle for driving through an area unnoticed. It didn't stop Trey from snickering.

"Where did you get this hunk of junk?"

"Found it parked in front of a farmhouse with a sale sign in the window. The farmer sold it to me for a hundred bucks."

"Yeah, well I think you overpaid."

"No way. It has a monster V8 and runs like a sewing machine. I had the windows tinted and rigged the back with everything I need for spy work. Park this baby on the side of the road, and nobody even notices, except maybe in Nichols Hills."

"Where we're headed ain't Nichols Hills," Trey said, "Although it's possible there are just as many thieves there."

Nichols Hills is an exclusive community surrounded by sprawling Oklahoma City. Some of the City's richest residents live there. As Buck and Trey both knew, in a state populated early by Boomers and Sooners, much of the wealth hadn't come honestly.

Trey directed them to a section-line road just north of the small town of Crescent. They turned on the rutted dirt road and headed west, crossing a creek on an old wooden bridge built in the thirties. A thick growth of blackjacks and sand plum bushes blocked the view on both sides of the creek. The dozen wild turkeys drinking from a shallow pool didn't bother hurrying away into the underbrush. Trey pointed to narrow blacktop as they crossed the creek. After making the turn, Buck pulled to the side of the road.

"You drive. Someone might recognize me if we get stopped." Crawling into the back, he grabbed a digital camera. "I'll take a few pics through the portholes."

Pard settled into the passenger's seat, wishing the window were open though not missing a thing.

"Good man," Trey said, giving him a friendly head rub before settling in behind the wheel and starting down the road.

They soon reached a tiny settlement made up of a few mobile homes, ramshackle buildings, and cars without tires sitting on cinder blocks. Choppers sat parked outside one of the trailers. Though the weather was warm, a thin strand of smoke puffed from a pipe in the trailer's ceiling.

"Meth house," Trey said. "I'd bet good money on it."

Buck snapped several pictures and then moved to the opposite side of the van.

"Did you notice no one has a mailbox?"

Trey laughed. "Hell, I doubt they know how to

read. They all have pet pit bulls in their backyards, though. Where to from here?"

"Follow the blacktop. This road would be red clay unless there were something important on the other end of it."

Trey continued through the little development, the last mobile home soon giving way to more blackjacks and scrub brush. About two more miles down the narrow road, they located what they were looking for: a holding pen for cattle. What they also found was something neither had suspected.

"Take a look," Trey said.

Gone were the ticky-tacky mobile homes, replaced by several acres of a well-run cattle operation. Steel fencing painted freshly white, encircled a holding pen that held a hundred or more mixed breed cattle. A large barn, feeding troughs and cutting pens painted the picture of a large and expensive cattle operation.

Behind the pens, a road led up the hill to an ornate wrought-iron gate and stone fence surrounding what appeared to be a palatial estate. A huge house centered a manicured and carefully landscaped lawn. Two black Cadillac limousines sat parked in front of the massive oak doorway, apparently waiting for someone inside.

"Holy shit!" Buck said.

"Do you see what I see?"

Buck had already noticed there were several different breeds present in the large holding pen.

"What do you make of it?"

"They must come from several herds. I don't know of a farm in Oklahoma that raises this many different breeds. I'm going to take some blood samples."

An armed man appeared from the barn when Trey, carrying his black bag, stepped out of the van. Dressed in jeans, worn boots, and cowboy hat, the man waved his shotgun in a menacing and convincing manner.

"Who the hell are you?"

"The vet. Your people called me about a bacterial infection. I need to check out these cows and take some blood samples."

"No one told me anything about a vet," the man said, still brandishing his shotgun. "I'll have to call it in."

"Fine. I'll get started because this will take a while."

The cowboy started to say something, thought better of it, took the phone from his checkered western shirt and dialed someone. Trey was already in the pen and collecting his first sample.

"My boss don't know nothing about you being here," the cowboy said after returning his attention to Trey.

"Because I'm from Texas. Part of the operation down there. I came up to help. It doesn't matter anyway. These cows are all infected, and I don't have the correct vaccine with me to treat them."

Trey vaulted the fence and headed for the van before the addled cowboy could question him further.

"Let's get the hell out of here," he said.

Buck didn't need prompting, pulling away as soon as Trey slammed the door. Even Pard sensed the need for urgency.

"Do any good?" Buck asked as he sped away.

"Only had time to take two samples. It may be enough to tell us what we need to know."

"If so, then we scored a home run."

"Not quite," Trey said as they rounded a corner and found their path blocked by two pickup trucks and several armed men.

"Let me do the talking," Trey said, getting out of the van. "What's the problem, fellas?"

"It's you that's got a problem, not us."

Greasy brown hair protruded from beneath

the unshaven man's cowboy hat as he stepped forward, brandishing an automatic weapon.

Trey raised his hands. "Hey, we're all on the same side here."

"Bullshit! No one has a clue who you are, or what you're up to."

"We all work for the same people. I'm up from Texas. Drove here from Wichita Falls this morning. Check it out. I wouldn't shit you."

Trey's lie was convincing, at least until the man from the barn came racing up behind them in his pickup, sliding sideways as he squealed to a halt in the road.

"They ain't none of ours," he said, as he bounded out of the truck.

The armed cowboys raised their weapons and started toward Trey. The noise of squealing tires and the acrid smell of burning rubber caused them to turn their attention to the van.

Buck had jammed the vehicle into reverse, pushing the pickup behind him into the ditch with the van's over-sized rear bumper. The truck's driver was in the line of fire, likely the only reason the cowboys didn't open up on Buck. Slamming the gearshift into first, he raced toward them, tires still squealing.

The cowboys and Trey tried to scatter. Before any of them had gone five feet, Buck tossed something out the window. An explosion of flashing light and ear-splitting sound knocked them to the ground. Buck and Pard sprang from the van, grabbing Trey and dragging him into the passenger seat. With the door still ajar, he wheeled the vehicle around, barely missing the pickup he had shoved into the ditch.

"What in holy hell?" Trey said, rubbing his ears and eyes. "This way's a dead end."

"You got a better idea?" Buck said as he gunned the van's big engine and raced away down the narrow blacktop.

Halfway back to the cattle pen, he wheeled the van off the road, down into the creek bed. A barely visible rutted dirt road followed the creek. Trey held on to his seat as the boxy vehicle bucked and swayed like a wild bull, waves of water splashing over the hood and windows as it plowed through the low-water crossing to the opposite side of the creek.

The path led up the hill to a treeless field where they saw the roof of an old abandoned barn in the distance. The wooden gate was shut, and Buck didn't bother stopping to open it, ramming the van straight through to the dirt road on the other side.

"What the hell did you explode back there?" Trey asked, still bumping the side of his head with his palm, trying to clear his ears.

"F.N.D.D."

"What the hell is that?"

"Flash and noise diversionary device—a stun grenade. One of my police friends got me a few. Never know when you might need one to get out of a jam."

Trey was still rubbing his eyes and shaking his head.

"Damn! I think I'm going to need a hearing aid."

"Sorry, buddy. I couldn't use it on the bad guys without including you. You'll be all right in an hour or so."

"Thanks for nothing," Trey said. "Where are we going?"

"There's a back road from Crescent to Guthrie. I'm cutting cross-country until I reach it. Is this going to be worth it?"

"If this operation is what I think it is, the blood samples will tell us plenty. Let's just hope those boys didn't get your tag number."

"You don't think this baby is tagged in my name, do you?"

Trey just moaned, leaned back in the seat, and closed his eyes.

The remaining trip to Sunset Farms proved uneventful, Trey feeling better as he exited the old van and climbed into his Wrangler.

"I'm going to get my people involved in this little cattle operation we discovered. Hopefully, we didn't spook them enough to start shutting down."

"And if they do?"

"There are still things we can learn. Someone owns or is leasing that facility. We'll follow the money. It'll lead us to the principals. I'll keep in touch. Meanwhile, stay off the road in your van."

Buck waved as Trey drove away from Sunset Farms. For the first time in several days, he performed the afternoon feeding, Pard at his heels. He showered and changed clothes. Georgia would be at Nick's having a drink, and he needed to see her.

"You stay and keep an eye on LaDona and her baby. I have to go to town, and they don't allow border collies in Nick's."

Chapter 20

It was after dark when Buck reached the Petro Place, parked the Navigator, and entered Nick's. The dimly lighted bar rocked with patrons listening to the piano player singing oldies. He found Georgia sitting alone in a booth, nursing a rum and Coke. She smiled when he slid in beside her.

"You look great, even with all your clothes on," she said.

He reddened, knowing to what she was referring.

"I can say the same for you. What's your connection with the place?"

"Lykaia is good for me. We all help each other. It's like the family I never had."

"But you don't live there."

"Residence isn't a requirement although I have an apartment I sometimes use."

"What is it that you do for Lykaia?"

"Anything they ask me," she said.

The piano player began singing Neil Diamond's *Sweet Caroline*, many of the club's patrons joining in.

"I was pretty stoned at the revel, though I can't forget seeing you and how hot you looked," he said.

"You were pretty hot yourself. I tried to get your attention. Lana had dibs on you. Maybe it's time we changed all that."

The noise level in Nick's was high, lights dim. No one seemed aware when she began rubbing his thigh. When Ronnie brought his Wild Turkey, she noticed.

"You two get a room," she said.

Buck managed to pull away from Georgia and sipped his whiskey until he caught his breath.

"Lana hired me to investigate an intruder. I didn't know it was going to turn into something I least expected."

"Uh huh," she said.

"It's just now dawning on me how much you resemble KK," he said, ignoring her skepticism. "You are both about the same height, your hair the same color and length."

"Like I said, we were roomies in college and best friends. People mistake us for sisters. It's fun playing the game. We usually hang together when Roy and Clayton are out of town."

"Did you know the man murdered on Clayton's ranch?"

Georgia's smile disappeared, and she nodded. "Frankie Boggs. He was like a brother to me. You remember the lingerie shows they used to have around town?"

"I heard about them."

"You went, just like every other horny oilie. Frankie and I would go for lunch. He worked for Clayton and helped me get my job with Crescent Oil."

"Sounds like you knew him well."

"He was supposed to be this year's Fertility Deity," she said.

"Did you see him before he was killed?"

Georgia had to think about it. "KK and I went two-stepping about the time it happened. You know Rustler's. The dance floor is gigantic."

Buck had spent many Friday nights in

Rustler's, a western-themed nightspot that featured live bull riding.

"Sure I do."

"KK said she told you about our adventure with the man who works for Roy. The one with fighting dogs and a big knife."

"Jimmy Quick. You saw him at Rustler's?"

"Frankie saw him first. He wanted to say something to him. KK and I were both frightened Jimmy might hurt him, so we split."

"To another bar?"

"We were already wasted and decided to call it a night. Since Jimmy knows where I live, Frankie drove us to Logan County and dropped us at the Lykaia front gate. KK and I spent the night there at my apartment."

"Did Quick follow you there?"

"Don't know. We were all a little looped and forgot about Jimmy soon as we left Rustler's."

"Maybe he waited until Frankie dropped you and KK off and then followed him back to Clayton's ranch."

Georgia thought about it a moment. "What are you getting at?"

"Do you have a picture of him?" he asked, evading her question.

"That's easy," she said, reaching for her cell phone. "I take pictures of everyone on my phone list. When they call, their picture shows up on the screen. Here he is with KK."

Buck studied the image of the handsome cowboy standing at least a foot taller than the smiling KK.

"Did you take this the night you two picked him up?"

Georgia nodded. "He likes to hang out at the Rock Bar with the bunch of degenerates who live north of Crescent."

Buck motioned Ronnie to bring him his tab.

"I'm going out there."

"Not to do anything crazy, I hope. You are a big man. Jimmy is bigger."

"I want to get a look at him. That's all."

"Leaving kind of early, aren't you, Cowboy?" Ronnie said as he stood to leave.

"Got to get my beauty rest," he said.

Georgia followed him through the crowded bar. "You aren't going without me."

"He knows you. It would cause a problem. I only want to get a look, not confront him."

"I don't care. I'm coming," she said, following him to the parking garage. "He won't bother me if I'm with you."

Buck turned her around, pointing her back toward Nick's.

"As much as I'd like to take you two-stepping, you would blow my cover. I'll catch you later."

Buck was barely out of the parking lot when he called Trey Calderham.

"Did I wake you?"

Trey laughed. "Beth usually works at the restaurant until it closes and I don't go to bed until she does. What's up?"

"Just wanted to ask how you were feeling, and to see if you had anything more on the cattle operation north of Crescent."

"My ears finally stopped ringing. I only see a few spots now when I close my eyes. Other than that, I think I'll live."

"That's good to hear," Buck said.

"We got the test results of the two blood samples I took. Like we thought, the cows were from farms around here, one as far away as Seminole County."

"Which means?"

"The operation is well organized. The cattle in the holding pen have one thing in common: they are all excellent breeding stock. We don't usually see this quality of cattle at the livestock sales. And Buck, the person who owns the ranch is Roy Dunlap."

"You kidding me?"

"Cattle rustling is something I don't kid about. So what are you up to?"

"On my way to the Rock Bar to check out the place."

"It's a hangout for the gang north of Crescent. Better wait and let me join you."

"No thanks."

What'll you do if one of those goons recognizes you?"

"I barely got out of the van. You did. That's why I need to do this alone."

"Not a good idea."

"It's the best one I have," he said, saying goodbye before Trey could protest further.

Leaving Nick's, Buck followed back roads to the Rock Bar, a local landmark that had received its name from its red sandstone façade. It was a place frequented by both rich and famous. The locals loved it. He pulled into the parking lot beside a midnight blue Dodge pickup. The vanity tag on the expensive truck said Quickster. There was either more money in dog and chicken fighting then Buck knew about, or else Jimmy Quick was into other things.

The parking lot brimmed with every imaginable vehicle, from expensive BMWs and Mercedes to old pickup trucks. Western swing music streamed from an open door in back, Friday night and payday the reason for the large crowd. Located far enough from Guthrie, the rustic bar didn't worry about fire ordinances or noise levels.

People crowded outside on the wooden deck, lighted with Japanese lanterns that overlooked the parking lot. Buck waded through the jeans and boot-clad young men and women, all clutching cold cans or bottles of beers.

Patrons inside stood shoulder-to-shoulder, either at the stained wooden bar or watching dancers two-stepping to the music of a live, loud band. Those lucky enough to have tables or booths ignored the masses pressing close to them.

"What'll you have?" the young bartender with slicked-down dark hair asked.

"Coors, in a bottle if you have it."

"The best way to drink it," he said, retrieving an icy Coors from the cooler beneath the counter. "I'm Jacob. I didn't catch your name."

"James," Buck said, giving him his real first name. "You have a nice crowd here tonight."

"Lots of pretty girls and even more horny Friday night cowboys."

Buck slammed his beer, sat the bottle on the polished countertop and nodded for another. Noise in the building lessened as the band finished its last song before taking a break. An attractive cowgirl, decked out in jean shorts, boots, crop top and Stetson, dropped a glass. When it shattered on the hardwood floor, applause and laughter erupted. Jacob moved away to pour a beer for another customer.

With his back against the bar, Buck scanned the crowd. It didn't take him long to spot Jimmy Quick, taller than most of the others in the crowded room. He was talking to two cowboys. With the band on break, many of the drinkers and dancers went outside to smoke and enjoy the mild weather. The two men with Quick went with them, though not before one of them pointed at Buck. He realized something was up when Quick sidled up beside him.

"I'm Jimmy," he said, not offering to shake Buck's hand. "Haven't seen you in here before."

"I'm James. Haven't been in lately."

Jimmy was tall, probably six-five, or six. The

muscles in his broad shoulders and barrel chest rippled through the fabric of his sky blue Western shirt, opulently decorated with epaulets and buckskin laces. Like Jacob, he had dark hair protruding from beneath his expensive cowboy hat.

As practically every person in the place did, he also wore jeans. Unlike most of the other patrons, his weren't Levi's or Wrangler's, but expensive, freshly pressed designer jeans. His hand-tooled exotic animal skin boots likely cost a month's wages for most men. They complemented his expensive Rolex and a huge diamond pinkie ring. Jimmy didn't skimp at the dentist's office either, flashing a set of freshly whitened teeth which looked almost too perfect.

A pretty woman with long bleached hair beneath her fancy Stetson stumbled through the crowd and grabbed his arm. Like Jimmy's diamond ring and gold Rolex, she was a flashy ornament. He didn't bother introducing her, and from her inane grin, Buck could tell she was either too soused or stoned to care. He had garnered Jimmy's attention, and the big cowboy apparently didn't want the woman around while he talked to him. Pulling a wad of hundreds from his jeans, he peeled off a bill and handed it to her.

"Too quiet in here," he said. "Go load the jukebox."

Jimmy patted her butt, earning him a suggestive wiggle as she took the Bennie and stumbled away through the crowd.

"Great piece of ass but she's as dumb as a stump," he said.

Buck was thinking seriously about making an early exit when Quick's two friends joined them. One of them was Johnny Crabtree. Buck held his breath, hoping he didn't remember him from Clayton's ranch.

"This is Johnny and Shorty. What's your name again?"

"James Tee," Buck said.

Johnny looked at him closely. "I know you from someplace.

"Not that I can remember."

"Where do you work?"

They all turned at once when an obviously inebriated voice said, "He's Clayton O'Meara's right-hand man. Isn't he gorgeous?"

Someone from the crowded dance floor joined them and edged in between Buck and Jimmy. The stunning woman put her arms around his neck and kissed him. It was KK.

Chapter 21

"What a lucky girl I am, finding the two best looking men in Oklahoma waiting at the bar for me. Any chance of a three-way?"

KK was the last person he'd expected to see, and his heart started to race. From Jimmy's expression, he was also surprised to see her.

"How do you know James?"

"I was only eighteen the first time he got into my pants. Everyone I know calls him Buck."

Buck just grinned and shook his head. KK was drunk and had already blown his cover. Grabbing her hand, he said, "I need to get her home. We'll talk again later."

Johnny Crabtree clamped down on his shoulder and said, "What's your hurry?"

"Sounds like we need to do some talking now," Quick said. "Let's take a walk outside."

Buck glanced around, wondering if he and KK could get through the crowd and out the door before a fight broke out.

They might have made it except Jimmy's blond girlfriend returned from the jukebox. Frowning when she saw KK, she grabbed the front of her blouse, ripping it until it gaped open, the buttons gone. She didn't leave it at that, dealing

KK's face a backhanded slap that snapped her head back.

Blood streamed from the corner of KK's mouth, though no tears appeared in her eyes. She returned the favor with a clinched fist. The blow sent Jimmy's girlfriend backward into the bar. It wasn't a knockout punch and only infuriated her. After wiggling her chin to assure her it wasn't broken, she launched into KK, rolling her to the dirty wooden dance floor.

"Catfight!" someone yelled, as the music stopped and the crowd closed around the two women, wrestling and clawing on the floor.

Jimmy forgot about Buck and turned his attention to the fight. Grabbing arms and shoulders, he shoved several verbose fight observers out of his way. When he made it to the center of the human ring, he grabbed the woman's arm and yanked her to her feet.

"You crazy bitch," he said as he popped her head back with a vicious backhand.

When Buck shoved his way to the center of activity, KK nailed him with a fist in the face as he tried to help her off the floor. He was reeling from the punch when Jimmy wheeled him around and took a roundhouse swing at him.

Buck ducked, though caught a violent knuckle to the chin. Realizing Jimmy was too big to fight straight up he dived for his knees and rolled him to the floor. A champion wrestler in high school, he knew the dirty bar floor was his element. His ploy almost succeeded. He was getting the best of the much larger man when someone kicked him in the side.

The fight was on with fists swinging and objects thrown. Jimmy was squeezing his neck, another man pummeling him with his fists when a gunshot sounded, knocking out the lights. Darkness engulfed the participants in the barroom brawl. The shooter nailed Jimmy with the butt of the pistol and then got into it with the other cowboy. Buck scooted around, looking for KK. He found her directly behind him, still fighting with Quick's blond girlfriend. Grabbing her arm, he pulled her through the riotous crowd and out the back door.

"Though I know you're having fun, I think those three cowboys want to kill me. Let's get the hell out of here. And hey, you pack a hell of a punch," he said as they raced away from the melee.

KK's blouse was in shreds as she sat in the front seat of the Navigator. Her arms tightly crossed, she had a big grin on her face.

"That was fun," she said. "Where are you taking me?"

"To Clayton's."

"Not the way I look. Your place."

"No way. You think I'm crazy? Clayton would kill me."

"Only if you tell him. I'm damn sure not."

Buck had dealt with the headstrong KK more than once and knew she wasn't going to take no for an answer. Finally squealing into Sunset Farms, he parked the car in front of the barn and led her upstairs to his suite.

"You never brought me here before," she said when he turned on the lights.

"Because Clayton's ex is as jealous as he is. Lucky for us, she's in Scotland."

When Pard came running, KK grabbed him, hugging him to her chest.

"Oh, how sweet!" she said. "What's his name?"

"Pard."

"I think he likes me," she said.

"I see that," he said.

"It is lucky Clayton's ex is in Scotland," she said, letting go of Pard and hugging Buck. "She'd rat us out for sure."

"There's going to be nothing to tell," Buck said. "There's the bedroom. I'm sleeping on the couch."

"Sure about that?"

"I can't do this, KK. I work for Clayton. I'm not going behind his back."

"You and your silly code of honor. I need a shower. At least point me in the direction of your bathroom."

"Through that door," he said.

KK returned with wet hair, draped only in a damp towel.

"Do you have something I can wear, or would you prefer me naked?"

Buck fished in a drawer, handing her an extra-large orange tee shirt that said OSU Cowboys.

KK took the soft cotton garment. "You and your precious team. When are you going to get a clue that OU not only plays the best football in Oklahoma but anywhere?"

"I'd advise you not to share your opinion with Clayton. Like I said, you can have the bed. I'll sleep on the couch after I take a shower."

He slipped into the bathroom and let hot water pour over his head and shoulders. After the stressful day, it felt like heaven. He luxuriated in the steamy stall when soft breasts pressed against his spine.

"You know we can't do this," he said.

Pushing her away, he draped a towel around his waist and returned to the front room.

"Leave me alone, KK. You know I don't have much willpower."

KK grabbed Pard and headed for the bedroom. "Fine, Pard will sleep with me.

<hr>

Sometime during the night, Pard had slipped out of the bedroom and had joined Buck on the couch. When he struggled off the couch and glanced in the mirror, he realized he had a black eye. His chin also ached, as did his ribs where someone had kicked him. KK was still asleep when he returned from feeding Pard and the horses.

"Gonna sleep all day?" he asked, shaking her shoulder.

"What I wouldn't mind doing all day doesn't involve sleeping."

"Forget it. Clayton is probably on his way home from Kansas City."

"You asshole, you sound like my mother."

"Are you trying to break up with Clayton?"

"No way. I love him."

"Like a father?"

"I have a father. I love Clayton as a man."

Irritated by his haranguing, she got out of bed and strolled naked to the bathroom, giving him an unobstructed view of her gorgeous rear end. When she returned, she had on one of his robes. He could also see she had her own black eye.

"I'm not sure who got the worst of the fight last night, you, or me."

"Not funny," she said. "What'll I tell Clayton?"

"That you missed him so much, you drove to your Mom's in Tulsa, and she had missed you so much you decided to stay a few days."

"You are good," KK said. "I haven't seen Mom in three months, and this is as good a time as any."

"How will you explain the black eye and bruises to her?"

She smiled for the first time. "I never lie to my mom. You wouldn't happen to have a blouse around, would you? Some wildcat ripped mine to shreds."

Buck didn't. LaDona did. She took KK under her wing, doctoring her scratches and applying makeup to mask the black eye. They were soon on their way back to the Rock Bar to retrieve her white Mercedes.

KK gazed out of her open window with pleading eyes as she prepared to head to Tulsa.

"You promise you'll never mention a word of this to Clayton?"

"I don't remember a thing."

He waved as she tooled away, then headed north to the brick-paved streets of Guthrie. The first territorial capital of Oklahoma was one of the starting points for the land run of 1889. It grew from nothing to a town with a population of ten thousand people in less than half a day. He parked the Navigator in front of the new police station.

The old Logan County Jail was little more than a medieval dungeon. Located below the County Courthouse, it was dilapidated and dangerous. Prisoners hated the old facility to the extent jailbreaks, and escape attempts had become endemic. Hagen had somehow found the money to change the scenario. The new Logan County Jail, a state-of-the-art facility, and model for the entire Country, even housed Federal prisoners.

Sheriff Hagen had not stopped with the jail, reaching out to the surrounding communities, offering help. Langston, a mostly black college community not far away, never had much of a law force. Hagen began assisting with their problems and provided much-needed aid when a tornado caused havoc in the tiny college town. The cute worker behind the bulletproof window of the dispatch office waved at Buck and buzzed him into the hall leading to administration, Hagen shaking his head when he entered his door without knocking.

"The prodigal son returns. Nice black eye."

"You should see the other guy," Buck said.

Buck was neither Hagen's son nor Hagen Buck's dad. Raised in foster homes, he'd never known his real father. Sheriff Hagen was married though had no children of his own, and they both enjoyed the illusion of being father and son.

"You owe me. Carol was feeling frisky for the first time in a month, and she didn't appreciate me leaving her alone to bail your butt out of a crack."

If Sheriff Hagen was Buck's surrogate dad, his wife Carol was his mom. He had eaten more Sunday dinners at her table than any place else he could think of, and it was Carol he always called when he needed advice about women.

"You were at the Rock Bar last night?"

"Trey called and warned me there might be trouble. Good thing he did because we had to break up a near riot when we got there. You didn't have anything to do with starting it, did you?"

"I left early."

"Uh huh! We arrested a dozen people." Hagen pivoted his chair around to face the pot behind him. After pouring two cups of black coffee, he handed one to Buck. "A stray bullet put your buddy Trey in the hospital."

The grin on Buck's face disappeared. "Trey was there?"

"He took a slug in the chest. He's at St. Clemmon's in critical condition."

"Who shot him?"

"Half the people in the place were packing. We found most of the weapons under the tables and in the parking lot where their owners tossed them when we showed up."

"Thanks, Sheriff. If I were you, I'd send Carol a dozen roses."

"Yeah, and if I were you, I'd put on a pair of sunglasses to cover that shiner. Hey, and call tomorrow and remind me about the roses."

<hr>

St. Clemmon's Hospital resided in the northwest part of Oklahoma City, and Buck had spent time there in the emergency room more than once. After learning Trey's location, he followed the halls to Intensive Care where he found Beth holding Trey's hand, IV's and medical instruments attached to his arms with tubes and wires. She backed away when he walked around the bed to hug her.

"How is he?"

"Alive, no thanks to you."

"I never planned for this to happen."

"Maybe that's your problem."

Buck let the remark pass. "Anything I can do?"

Beth's anger disappeared. Putting her arms around him, she began to sob.

"I'm so frightened."

Her words aroused Trey from his drug-induced stupor. "I'm in the hospital one minute, and you've already got your hands on my girl."

Buck squeezed his shoulder. "I know we're friends. You didn't have to take a bullet for me."

"If I hadn't, you probably wouldn't have a head. Your good buddy was about to chop it off with his big knife."

"I should have known it was you who shot out the lights and nailed Jimmy Quick. If you count fishing me out of Guthrie Lake, this makes the second time you've saved my life."

"Third counting Pandora's," Trey said, managing a weak smile. "Can you take Beth and get her something to eat? She hasn't left the room since I got here."

"You trust me with her?"

"No way, Cowboy. I trust her."

Trey's eyes closed when Buck and Beth, gently shutting the door behind them, left the hospital room. They were only a few steps down the hall when Beth's eyes began tearing.

"His doctor thinks he will pull through. There are so many things that still can happen."

Buck led her to the elevator and then down a narrow hallway to the cafeteria. Institutional food is never wonderful. St. Clemmon's was tolerable. Buck followed her through the line, making sure she filled her plate. After an amorous night with KK, he was famished, piling his own plate with catfish and French fries.

"Trey will be fine," he said between bites. "He was my best friend growing up, though we had our share of blows. Believe me, when I tell you, there's not a tougher hombre in Oklahoma."

Beth smiled for the first time. "Trey is the man of my dreams. I'll die if I lose him."

"You aren't going to lose him, I promise you."

"I could kill the monster who did this to him."

She shook her head when he said, "Sheriff Hagen seemed to think he caught a random bullet."

"The knife wound wasn't random."

"What knife wound?"

Beth began sobbing again. "Someone carved the letter Q into his back."

Buck managed to calm Beth again. The news about Trey's knife wound struck him like a sledgehammer to the chest. If he'd had doubts before about who had questioned Hector and LaDona, he no longer did. It made him wonder why the Sheriff hadn't told him about Trey's deliberate disfigurement.

He and Beth had swirled cones of chocolate and vanilla ice cream before returning to the elevators. She stopped when they reached them, grasping his hand and sobbing again. Buck held her until her tears abated.

"Trey'll finish the investigation himself when he gets out of here. Maybe you should go home and get some rest."

"I'm not going anywhere except back upstairs."

Buck watched the elevator doors close, thinking seriously about finding Jimmy Quick, taking him someplace secluded and screwing him up.

He sat in the Navigator for ten minutes stewing over what he should do about Jimmy Quick before leaving the hospital parking lot. The big man was good with a knife. It didn't mean he'd killed Frankie Boggs or cut the letter Q in Trey's back. Maybe not, though Buck no longer harbored any doubt.

Chapter 22

Buck left the hospital with a heavy heart. Beth's accusing stare had burned a hole in his soul, and he couldn't help but feel guilty about involving Trey in a case that had almost gotten him killed. Worse, the letter Q Quick had carved into Trey's back would haunt him forever. Needing someone to talk to about it, he turned the Navigator around and headed toward Lycaia.

Buck opened the moon roof, the weather warm and a persistent breeze setting up an arboreal wave as it whistled through the trees. The two familiar Lykaia cops met him at the gate in their electric squad car.

"No one told us you were coming. We'll have to clear it with Lana," the older woman said.

When they opened the door at the police station, they found Esme and Princess waiting for them.

"He's here to see me," she said.

The two cops shared a glance as if to question Esme's assertion. Thinking better of protesting, they returned to their car and drove away. Buck gave Princess a head rub.

"Thanks for covering for me," he said.

"No cover. We were waiting for you."

"You kidding? I'm not even sure myself why I'm here."

Esme took his hand. "You have questions; I have answers. Have you eaten?"

"My friend is in the hospital with a gunshot wound. I had something to eat in their cafeteria."

"Your friend will be fine," she said.

"How do you know?"

"The same way I knew you were coming here. Trust me, even the cut on his back will heal and fade away with time."

"You're making me feel better, even if I'm not sure I believe you."

"Like I said, trust me."

They found the teepee dark, only the flame from the hearth fire lighting it. Shadows danced on the walls as Esme sat on the floor blanket, Princess sprawling beside her. When Buck joined them, Esme began rubbing a soothing and aromatic ointment on his black eye.

"Seems as though we've played this song before," he said as she pulled off his shirt, checking him for wounds.

"You're a project," she said.

After draping his shoulders with a blanket, she recovered a large object wrapped in a cloth from the corner of the teepee. It glowed brightly when she exposed it, sitting it on the blanket in front of the fire. Buck reached to touch it but drew back immediately.

"What the hell?" he asked.

"A Mayan crystal skull," she said. "Carved from a seam of Mexican quartz."

A prism of colored light danced from the fractures and imperfections in the skull.

"It's magnifying the light from the fire," he said.

Esme shook her head and held the crystal skull away from the flame. If anything, it glowed even brighter.

"The skull has a life of its own. You can see the future in its eyes if you know how to interpret the fire coming from them. Take it and feel its power."

Buck took the skull from her, amazed at how much it weighed. When a vibration ran up his arms, through his shoulders and the back of his neck, he realized she wasn't kidding. He quickly handed it back to her.

"That's the strangest thing I've ever felt," he said. "Still, the light must be coming from the flames of the fire."

Esme didn't answer, extinguishing the flames with a few handfuls of dirt. Even in the relative darkness of the teepee, the crystal skull continued to pulsate with the glow of colorful light.

"There's no battery," she said. "The skull is at least a thousand years old. Take it and look if you don't believe me."

"I believe you," he said. "It's just that I've never seen anything so strange."

"The universe conceals many secrets of which most mortals are unaware."

Esme wrapped the crystal skull in its cloth, put it away, and then restarted the fire.

"Something smells good," Buck said. "Are you cooking?"

"Thought you said you weren't hungry."

"I could eat a bite," he said.

Esme scooped something into a wooden bowl from the pot dangling over the rekindled fire. She handed it to Buck, along with a big, wooden spoon with which to eat it. He smiled after savoring the first taste.

"Like it?"

"It's wonderful. What's in it?"

"Porridge of squash, walnuts, and Indian corn."

"Delicious. Sure it didn't come from Lana's

restaurant."

"I not only cook my own food, I either grow or gather it myself."

"Well, this is wonderful. What now?" he asked after eating the last tasty morsel.

"A nap. I sense you're weary and you'll need all the strength you can muster before the night ends."

Esme draped a blanket over him after he'd curled up on the comfortable pallet.

"Where are you going?"

"Princess and I have business to attend to. We'll wake you when we return."

Buck hadn't realized how much sleeping on his lumpy couch, the previous night's fight, and dealing with Trey's injuries had taken out of him. Esme and Princess were barely outside the flap of the teepee when his eyes closed, and he fell into a deep sleep. He remained that way for several hours because it was dark outside when Esme returned and shook his shoulder. Kristy and Princess were with her.

"I hated to wake you," she said. "You were sleeping like a baby."

"I must have needed it. I feel better than I have in days. What's up?" he asked when he saw Kristy.

"Lana wanted to know what you're doing here. She sent me to find out."

"Consulting Esme. She's helping me with my cattle rustling investigation."

"Lana can help," Kristy said. "She's connected, and not just in Oklahoma. I'll speak to her about it."

"Is it possible she could compromise the investigation? I can't afford to take that chance."

"Lana understands security. She won't compromise your investigation. Tell me about your problem?"

"Someone is stealing oil and cattle from

Clayton O'Meara. He suspects Roy Dunlap, his business partner. Dunlap has a ranch north of Crescent that's adjacent to a cattle pen operation loaded with quality cows from several ranches in Oklahoma."

"How do you know that?" Kristy asked.

"My friend Trey Calderham is a registered agent for the Texas and Southwestern Cattle Raisers Association. We visited the cattle operation, and Trey took blood samples."

Kristy fished around in her purse for a pad of paper and began taking copious notes.

"What else?" she asked.

"Trey took a bullet in a bar fight. A man named Jimmy Quick carved the letter Q on his back. Quick works for Dunlap and is probably the murderer of the cowboy killed at Clayton's ranch."

She finally stopped asking questions and returned the pad and pencil to her purse.

"I have enough here," she said.

"Would you like something to eat?" Esme said.

"Not tonight," Kristy said. "I'm meeting Lana and Sara for a briefing over dinner at the Tiers. I'll talk to her about your investigation."

"Thanks," Buck said.

Outside the teepee, dark clouds floated overhead. Lightning flashed across the skyline, followed by distant thunder. Rain began sprinkling their shoulders as he held the teepee flap for the departing Kristy. What had begun as a light sprinkle of rain changed abruptly into a heavy deluge.

Esme, her arm around Beauty, waited on a colorful rug facing the small fire that always seemed to burn inside the teepee. The poor animal was shivering, her body flinching every time thunder rumbled.

"My big brave wolf dog is a baby when it comes to thunderstorms."

Buck joined them on the blanket, luxuriating in the warmth of the open fire. Beauty whimpered once and then changed positions, squirming to place her body into the space between Esme and Buck. Despite the raging storm, he felt secure and cozy inside the teepee. Beauty's incessant quivering abated as she drew as close to him as physically possible. Esme noticed.

"I'm sending Beauty to stay with you next time we have a storm," she said.

"Better idea. Next time it storms, I'll show up over here."

"I like that idea," Esme said.

The tempest continued for most of the night, rain falling, stopping, and then starting again. Beauty didn't join Esme and Buck in the sleeping pallet though she was never far away. She was by his side when he awoke the next day.

"Morning, Miss Beauty," he said, hugging her big neck. "Where's your mama?"

As if understanding Buck's question, she left the dim teepee, soon returning with Esme.

"I don't know how you ever get any work done, sleeping as late as you do."

Buck glanced at his old Rolex. "It's only seven."

"I've been up since five."

"Maybe you didn't expend as much energy as I did last night."

"You definitely know how to warm a girl up," she said.

The rest of the morning included scrambled eggs wrapped in a tortilla along with a pot of black coffee Esme brewed over an open flame. By midmorning, they were naked in the hot tub. Sitting across from her in muted light of a cloudy day, Buck took pleasure in her exotic beauty and strange tattoo whose meaning at which he could only guess. Wet from their soak, her long hair accented dark eyes as it draped her lithe back and shoulders. Oklahoma was originally Indian Territory, and even today has the largest population of Native Americans in the United States. Even so, few full-blood Indians now remain, even in Oklahoma. From her appearance, Esme could pass as a full blood Native American.

She grinned when he asked, "What tribe are you?"

"What makes you think I'm an Indian?"

"Just a guess. You do live in a teepee, cook on an open fire, and wear a breechcloth."

"Archeologists call us Mississippians."

"Never heard of that tribe."

"Because there aren't many of us left."

"How many?"

"Just me."

Buck's mouth opened. No words issued forth. He finally said, "You're kidding, right?"

"I'm very serious. You've heard of the Spiro Mounds?"

Everyone in Oklahoma knew about the Spiro Mounds. Buck had visited once while in grade school and had never forgotten the only remaining location from one of the most important Pre-Colombian archeological sites in the United States.

"I didn't know there were any Mississippians left. Where is your family from?"

He sensed he'd overstepped his bounds when she responded coolly to his question.

"Why is it important to you?"

"I was just looking at you, thinking how to drop dead gorgeous you are, and wondering what sort of wonderful family heritage you must have to have endowed you with such brains and beauty."

Esme smiled despite herself. "It's easy for me to recognize your heritage, Mr. Blarney Stone."

Esme pushed him away when he tried to put

his arms around her.

"What?"

"There is a time and place for everything. This is neither the time nor the place, so keep your big hands to yourself."

Buck knew a rebuke when presented with one. "Sorry, the old demon testosterone was trying to take charge again."

"Oh, you mean something else controls your brain from time to time?"

"Funny."

Esme rolled her dark eyes. "Yes, we're without clothes in the hot tub, though you have seen me naked on more than one occasion. We have other things to talk about."

"Such as?"

Reaching behind her, she grabbed a ceremonial cloud blower. After lighting it and taking a puff, she handed it to him.

"The answers you seek. You must take a spirit walk, and I cannot accompany you."

<hr>

Barefoot and dressed only in a breechcloth, Buck followed a path, Beauty by his side. They were in a forest unlike any he'd ever seen, the trees surrounding them gigantic, probably never cut. There was no underbrush or growth of vines beneath the trees, so tall and massive they blocked most of the light from the sun.

Ground fog rolled slowly across their loamy pathway, rising as high as the base of lower limbs on the massive trees. The result was a dreamlike aura made even more surreal by effervescent violet and purple light filtering through the branches. There was only silence, and when Buck spoke to Beauty, his words sounded hollow and muted, his voice resonating from somewhere deep in his lungs.

"Where are we, girl?" he asked, not feeling his

lips move.

Fog swirled in rivulets around their legs as they continued along. Buck had no sense of where they were going. It didn't seem to matter; his head swam from the drug he had smoked in the pipe. Beauty seemed to know where she was going and he followed her.

He soon realized they were not alone. Giant butterflies and even larger moths fluttered with wings of iridescent green and azure through the rolling fog, their colorful appendages setting up rippling patterns of clashing colors as they parted the rolling mist engulfing them. When they reached a barely discernible path, Beauty stopped and looked up at him.

She didn't react when he asked, "Which way, girl?"

Pulsating light emanated from the emerald-colored wings of a creature that looked like a giant Luna moth. Beauty didn't start when it appeared in their path and then disappeared into the rolling mist. The two travelers continued along the trail, as subliminal as real. Buck had the sense he was floating and not walking. Perhaps he was.

They continued for an interminable time, going many miles or perhaps only a few hundred yards. It didn't matter because all sense of time, space and distance had abandoned his psyche. When they reached the intersection of two paths, Beauty sat on the ground and waited for him. Again, he realized he would have to make the decision.

As he glanced around, wondering what to do, a slight breeze began wafting away the fog. The air around him filled with a visage of light bursting forth in small explosions of color and then disappeared like wraiths in the night. Buck glanced at Beauty again. She offered no direction for his ever-increasing feelings of doubt. The sound of a crow caused him to glance into the trees. The bird was large, its wings a luminous black that shimmered like black paint in a stirred can.

The crow didn't answer when Buck asked, "Which path?"

Watching it fly away, he wondered if it were a sign, telling them the path to follow. An ebony feather lost by the bird twirled slowly to earth, its quill pointing opposite the direction from where the crow had flown. Picking up the feather and putting it in his hair, Buck and Beauty took that path, soon reaching a stream.

Water appeared to flow almost like a computer simulation, its movement created by illusions of the mind rather than actual motion. When Buck touched it, his toe ignited a burst of green and red. He and Beauty waded into the icy water, their movement sending soundless explosions of vivid color flashing around their legs.

The path widened and narrowed, and then widened again, exotic plants with colorful flowers blooming on either side. There was no sound, not even the crunch of leaves beneath their feet as they trod the path. Trees began giving way to a distant clearing. Sensing they were near their destination, Buck and Beauty picked up their pace.

Rolling fog parted as they entered a clearing abutting a large lake, its water so clear and free of ripples, he could see fish swimming just below its surface. A golden loon soared overhead, suspended almost motionless in a thermal updraft. They walked along the water's edge, sometimes following its cobbled bank, and sometimes wading in its warm shallows.

Raindrops sprinkled their shoulders, evaporating as fast as it fell. The sky turned cloudy, and Buck watched lightning bolts race across the darkening sky. The light show was noiseless, unaccompanied by thunder.

The soundless storm continued for what seemed a very long time when suddenly rain and lightning ceased. The sky cleared and lightened to reveal a rainbow that breached the heavens. Purple Martins soared overhead, chasing invisible insects. As Buck turned a corner leading to a cove in the lake, he somehow understood they had reached their destination.

A log cabin sat near the center of the cove, wisps of smoke rising from its thatched roof. Solid limestone rose up a hundred feet behind the cabin, and a lone eagle soared high above them. Buck glanced at it, and then at the winding path of colorful cobbles leading to the cabin door. When Beauty circled a spot and lay in the soft sand, Buck somehow knew he must enter the cabin alone. He did so, not bothering to knock first.

Pungent odors of herbs and burning wood met his nostrils as he eased through the creaky door, the dimly lit room revealing the outline of a man sitting on the ground beside a small fire.

"Come in my son," the man said without bothering to turn around. "Join me by the flame."

Buck sat on the ground beside him and warmed his hands. You knew I was coming?"

The man was a very old Indian, his hair snowy white, as were his eyebrows, his prominent brow crowning a regal Aztec nose. Gold ringlets hung from his stretched earlobes. The color of his skin was deep reddish brown, as Buck had never seen.

"You made it."

"You expected me?"

"For many days now."

"Where is this place?"

"It is the edge of the world."

In Buck's state of altered consciousness, the old man's answer didn't seem particularly odd.

"Why am I here?"

"For answers."

"I don't even know the questions."

"Few people do."

"I have never experienced a place such as this. It's almost like I'm in a dream."

"Maybe you are," the old man said.

"But I am fully aware of everything around me. If you cut me, I'm sure I would bleed. This is real."

"Even dreams are real."

"Then am I dreaming?"

The old man didn't answer his question. "You have passed every test so far. There are more."

"What tests?"

"You were wise not to follow the crow. You are also wise enough to believe in omens." He pointed to the feather still in Buck's hair. "Omens do not always signal something good or bad. Sometimes they simply indicate the path you should follow."

"What now?"

"You must drink from the black cup."

An earthen vat sat beside the fire, and the old man produced a black cup made from what looked like a conch shell. Engraved symbols with meanings Buck didn't grasp decorated the cup and reminded him of Esme's tattoo. He dipped it into the vat, and then held it to his lips and drained it. When the last drop dribbled from the corners of his mouth, he plunged it again into the vat.

"Now you must drink," he said, handing Buck the ceremonial cup.

Dark brown, almost black liquid filled the vessel. Buck took it and put it to his lips, frowning from the bitter taste as he drained it. The old man nodded his approval. Dipping the cup into the vat again, he drank all of it for the second time, then filled it again and handed it to Buck.

Seeing his grimace, the old man smiled. "Are you okay?"

"This tastes awful, what is it?"

"Asi, the tea of truth."

Whatever was in the drink caused Buck's head to buzz and his body to shake. The reaction grew more intense after two more cups of the hot liquid.

"Asi removes all sin and purifies the soul. Drink more," he said, handing Buck yet another cup of the strong liquid.

The old man finally sat the black cup on the ground and lit a ceremonial pipe. After a long pull, he handed it to Buck. The first puff he took was so strong it almost caused his eyes to cross. Grinning when he saw Buck's grimace, the old man led him outside. Beauty didn't follow them as they took a narrow pathway to the top of the sheer rock cliff behind the cabin. The old man stopped at the edge of the cliff where it overlooked the pristine lake. Bending forward, he closed his eyes and vomited over the precipice.

"If you are to find wisdom, you must purge yourself of whatever evil lives in your body."

Buck approached the precipice, bent forward, and vomited the strong black beverage out of his system. As he wiped his mouth with the back of his hand, he realized the old man was still holding his other arm. He continued doing so, leading him back down the path and into the cabin.

Returning to his place beside the fire, the old man relit the pipe and puffed it.

"Now you are cleansed and can see the truth."

"I see nothing. Please help me."

The old Indian handed Buck the cloud blower and waited until he puffed the strong tobacco.

"You are in danger. You have wandered into the realm of two evil spirits."

"The panther?"

"Yes, at least in one of his guises. The panther, or the spirit the big cat sometimes represents, is a shape-shifter. He has come to your world to avenge a wrong. You are not the target, though you are still in danger."

"Beauty saved me from the cat. She is fearless."

"Beauty embodies perfect goodness; the single element evil can never overcome. She saved you once. She cannot help you if she is not around."

"You spoke of two evils."

"Yes, one ancient evil spirit has taken the form of a man in your world. He is not really a man."

The old Indian nodded when Buck asked, "The one called Jimmy Quick?"

"He senses you are after him and he will kill you if he can."

Buck stared at the old man with dilated eyes. "What is your name?"

"That is not important."

"Then at least tell me if this is a dream."

"No my son, this is very real."

Chapter 23

Buck awoke in Esme's teepee, the old Indian's words still echoing in his head. He had many questions. She was heading for the door before he had a chance to ask.

"Where are you going?"

"I have morning duties."

"What duties?" he asked.

"Greeting the dawn on the eastern perimeter for one," she said. "Today is a holy day. I won't return until after dark. Will you be here when I return?"

"Don't know," he said. "I have a few things on my plate I need to clean off first."

Buck returned to Sunset Farms to feed Pard and the horses. It was already mid-afternoon when he discovered he'd left his cell phone in the Navigator. He had ten missed calls when he finally checked them. One was from Beth, and it was the first call he returned.

"The doctors sent Trey home last night. He wants to see you."

"Great news. Is it okay if I come by?"

"I'd be upset if you didn't. Come have lunch

with him at the Pendant."

Buck glanced at his watch. "It's a little late for lunch."

"No problem," she said. "I have an in with the cook."

"I'm on my way."

It was closer to dinner than lunch when he finally joined Trey at a booth in Beth's Azure Pendant restaurant. Buck had hugged him before he had a chance to say anything.

"Stop it, Cowboy. I hurt bad enough as it is. You're going to break my ribs."

"I should break your neck for getting shot."

"Boys, boys, if you two are going to squabble, then take it to the streets."

"Uncle," Buck said, raising his arms. "I'm too hungry to fight, and it wouldn't be much of a challenge whipping up on an incapacitated man."

"That's the only way you'll ever whip me," Trey said.

Buck sat in the booth as Beth shook her head and returned to the kitchen. The interior of the Azure Pendant resembled a cozy hacienda, complete with Mexican tile floor, beamed ceiling, and an open hearth in the center. Hanging ferns and large potted plants helped separate the tables and provide a feel of spacious dining. Trey was drinking iced tea.

"Tea, huh? You really aren't feeling good, are you?"

"Doc said no alcoholic beverages while I'm on drugs and the Enforcer is making sure of it," Trey said, nodding toward Beth as she returned with a cold mug of Tecate for Buck.

"Sorry, Pal, I'll enjoy this one for both of us. You look good. How do you feel?"

"Not too bad, except for the new tattoo on my back."

"Beth said you have some information."

"New info, though not necessarily good. We were able to trace the ownership of the cattle-holding facility to a nondescript LLC that doesn't seem to have any principals. We're still trying to track the ownership. Whoever formed it knows how to work the system."

"It isn't part of Dunlap's ranch?"

"That's what's strange. It appears connected to the ranch and the people who work there work for Dunlap. Someone has gone to great lengths to keep the two entities separate, at least for the record."

"Where are all the cows going?"

Trey sipped his tea before answering. "Don't have a clue. I have agents watching the facility."

"There are too many coincidences here for Dunlap not to be involved."

"I agree. Maybe you should check out his office and have a look at his files."

"You want me to break into his office?"

"Why not, you're pretty good at slipping locks. If he is involved, he has to keep books on the operation somewhere, and he spends most of his time at Crescent Oil."

They dined on sour cream enchiladas, and Buck drank another Tecate before saying goodbye to Trey and Beth. Many of the city's workers were already making their way to various watering holes around town. A crowd had begun gathering in the Azure Pendant's bar as Buck headed toward the Petro Place, hoping to hatch a plan to get a look inside Roy Dunlap's office.

Most of Crescent Oil had already shut down for the day, headed for Nick's. The boisterous crew welcomed him when he joined them. Georgia was alone and well into her cups. He noticed when she glanced at him with a drunken grin.

"Hi, baby. I've been missing you," she said when she saw him.

"Where's Roy?"

"Horse races in Hot Springs. I think he has another girlfriend over there."

"He's crazy if he does because she can't be as pretty as you are."

"Pretty doesn't matter with you men. You'd stick your dick in a Twinkie if you thought it would make you feel good."

"You're abusing the wrong man," he said. "I've never done you wrong, have I?"

Georgia touched his cheek and smiled. "Not yet. The night's still young."

"I'm not that way," he said.

"You're really cute, and it makes me want to do something dirty with you."

The two Tecate's had given him a buzz, along with the Wild Turkey and water Ronnie brought him. Georgia was practically in his lap, her body heat already elevating his own temperature. His plan to get into Dunlap's office came together when she blew in his ear.

"You're mad at Roy."

"I'd like to scratch his eyes out," she said.

"If you're serious, I have an idea for you to get even with him."

"I'm all ears," she said.

"Roy must be an idiot to leave a gorgeous woman like you alone. We need to make him pay. Let's do it on his desk and really give him something to think about."

Georgia grinned. "I like it."

Almost everyone in the Crescent Oil group noticed when Buck and Georgia left the bar, smiling, and waving as if they were in on some secret. He liked her soft warmth as she groped him in the elevator on the way upstairs. He didn't intend to have sex with Georgia. He only needed her to get into Roy's office so he could access his computer. Still, it didn't stop him from feeling like a heartless bastard for using her to accomplish his goal.

"I can't remember the code with your tongue in my mouth," she said as she punched in numbers at the front door.

Despite her admonition, the light on the keypad turned green, and she entered with no alarm sounding. Buck held her hand as she led him down the hall to Dunlap's office.

"Roy is a stickler for security. He will die when he realizes we were in his office after hours."

Georgia chuckled as she punched in Roy's code. They were barely inside his office before she had strewn half her clothes across the expensive Oriental carpet. Buck wondered as she began emulating a person possessed by a sexual demon if he would accomplish anything other than unbridled sex with a scorned woman. She loosened his belt and unbuttoned his jeans, stopping abruptly when she sensed he wasn't cooperating.

"What's wrong?"

"This sounded like a good idea downstairs. Now, I just can't do it."

"You think I don't know why we're here? I want you as much as you want me."

"I'm having a conscience attack. This just isn't right."

"To hell with your conscience! All my friends downstairs saw us leave together. Every one of them thinks we're having sex right now. I'm going to do some naughty things to you, and you are going to like it. When we go back downstairs, and everyone is looking at us, I want your tongue halfway down my throat and your hands on my ass. You got it, cowboy?"

"Yes ma'am," Buck said as Georgia continued working on him

Several minutes of intense passion followed

Georgia's admonition. Buck, finally remembering where they were, and why they were there, pushed her gently away.

"We have to stop this. Someone's going to catch us," he said.

"That's the point," she said.

"Uncle," he said, sitting up and rubbing his forehead, his senses slowly starting to return to normal.

Georgia fished in her purse until she found her cell phone. With their clothes in disarray and half-naked bodies on display, she extended her arm and took a picture. Satisfied, she directed it to her email address. Cranking up Roy's computer, she downloaded the picture to the desktop, leaving it as the background on his screen.

"You know his password? Buck asked, beginning to recover.

"I know everything about him, including his underwear size."

"Then what is it?"

"His underwear size?"

"His password."

"Cowdaddy."

"Roy will fire you when he sees this."

"Cards laid are cards played," she said, her words a drunken slur.

Georgia was done, both literally and figuratively. Buck wrestled her clothes back on her as best he could and returned with her to the basement bar. She was feeling the effects of the alcohol she had consumed. When they joined the Crescent crew, she forgot about Buck's tongue in her mouth and his hands on her ass.

"She's had it," he told Sandy. "Mind taking her home? I have some more work to do upstairs."

"Looks to me like you've already done some work upstairs," she said, grinning.

Despite their ribbing, Sandy and Ty agreed to

drive Georgia home. Buck returned to the Crescent Oil offices. He'd watched Georgia use Roy's keypad and hoped the excitement hadn't caused him to forget the code. The door opened with no problem, and he shut it behind him before proceeding to the computer.

The screen fired to life again when he entered the password, the mostly naked picture of him and Georgia greeting him as Roy's new screen background. He changed the background and deleted the picture from the computer. No need tipping Dunlap off someone had accessed his private information.

Most of the files on the computer concerned Crescent Oil business. He soon learned Dunlap kept two sets of oil well pumping and gauging reports, one showing actual production, the other altered production. It was apparent he was stealing his own company's oil. Try as he might, Buck could find no reference to a cattle operation, illegal or otherwise. Roy was more cautious than he had thought. Maybe he wasn't as cautious with his emails.

Buck clicked on Roy's desktop email basket, trying to access it using the password cowdaddy. Cowdaddy didn't work, nor cowdaddy1. Cowdaddy10 did. He checked Roy's emails. Since Dunlap's email server wasn't web-based, he knew he would have to glean what information he could before leaving the office.

The Petro Place had a night watchman. Buck had met the young man on several occasions. He didn't want to explain what he was doing in Roy's office, so he began work at once. Dunlap took care of his emails in a meticulous manner, all sorted alphabetically in folders. One folder labeled Molasse had more than a hundred entries, many referring to the sale of cattle. Buck had a tiny jump drive attached to his key chain he used to store information from his computer. Inserting it into the USB port, he copied the entire Molasse file. He was busy visually scanning some of the other files when he heard someone outside the door.

It didn't matter who it was, either the janitor or the night watchman. He would have some explaining to do if they found him sitting at Roy's computer in the dark. He didn't wait for the door to open. Turning off the computer screen, he crawled under Roy's desk, pulling the fancy office chair in front of him. The door opened. No one entered, cluing Buck it was probably the night watchman. The janitor would have turned on the lights to empty the trash and vacuum the floor. He held his breath until the person in the hall shut the door.

He listened to footsteps padding down the hallway, stopping periodically to randomly check an office door. Hoping the folder he had copied contained valuable information, he waited a moment to make sure no one was in the hall. When he opened the door, he got the surprise of his life.

Chapter 24

The person in the hallway was as surprised to see him, as he was to see her.

"Georgia, what in the hell are you doing here?"

"I got to thinking about the picture we left on Roy's computer screen and decided I needed to delete it."

Buck lowered his eyes and rubbed his forehead. "I beat you to the punch."

Still woozy from all the alcohol she had consumed, she didn't question his story. Instead, she said, "Good, because I would just die if Roy had found our picture."

"It's gone. I'll show you if you like."

"I trust you," she said, making him feel like an even bigger heel than he already did.

"Sandy said she would take you to your house."

"She did. I caught a cab back because I was shaking when I woke up on the couch."

"It's all right now. I'll take you home."

Georgia huddled against the passenger-side door during the short ride, her arms tightly folded.

"You know what we did doesn't mean anything to me. I was only using you to get back at Roy. Can you forgive me?"

"You were drunk, and I took advantage of you."

"You are full of yourself, Buck McDivit. I haven't had sex with anyone I didn't want to since I was seventeen, no matter how drunk I was."

"That's good to know. I wouldn't want to come between you and Roy."

This time Georgia laughed. "I'm not ready to call it quits with him yet, though I'm this close," she said, measuring an inch with her thumb and forefinger.

"When you decide to quit him, I know someone you might like."

"You're a real hunk. No offense, I like older men."

"Not me, someone else."

"I'll keep it in mind."

Buck let the subject drop. "Have you ever heard of the Molasse Company?"

Georgia nodded. "I didn't tell you everything I know about Jimmy Quick."

"Oh?"

"He works for Molasse, and Roy. Roy does business with them."

"What kind of business?"

"You know how secretive he is. When I asked him, he got defensive and told me it wasn't any of my business."

"What does Quick do for them?"

"Provides security, sort of like a bodyguard. It must be important because they pay him lots of money."

"Even more than he makes fighting dogs and chickens?" Georgia shook her head. "Did Roy know about Frankie Boggs?"

Georgia nodded. "Roy doesn't want to marry me. He doesn't want anyone else to either."

"You had an affair with Frankie?"

"We were close friends and had sex from time

to time."

"And KK?"

"KK and I are best friends. She likes who I like, and vice-versa. Neither of us are virgins. Stop looking at me like I'm some sort of a whore."

"Sorry," he said, turning away. "I'm not exactly a saint myself."

"That's a fact," she said. "I've known Billy goats less horny than you."

She laughed aloud when he said, "Baa!"

Georgia wouldn't let him walk her to the door of her house. She stood outside the Navigator, standing on her tiptoes to kiss him goodnight through the window.

"Did you delete the picture of us off your cell phone," he asked.

"The caller's picture shows up on the screen when my phone rings. I can hardly wait until you call," she said with a wanton grin.

Buck suddenly had more information than he could digest and needed someone to talk to about it. Sheriff Hagen and his wife Carol were the closest he'd ever come to having a real mother and father. Hagen had rescued him from juvenile detention, inviting him to spend the weekend at his little farm outside of Guthrie.

Sheriff Hagen had taught him how to ride a horse. It was his wife Carol who had instructed him how to be a better person. When Buck needed motherly advice, Carol Hagen was the only person who could come close to filling the bill. After stopping long enough to pick up Pard, he headed the Navigator North on I-35 toward Hagen's farm.

"Miss me, Pard?" he asked.

The wet tongue on his face and the little dogs wagging tail were all the answer he needed.

The night was warm. Opening the sliding roof, he stared up at the sky. Stars and moon were clearly visible. Rapidly moving clouds, blowing in from the southwest, had begun covering them. He shut the moon roof when a light sprinkle of rain began to fall. Not bothering to turn on the radio, he let darkness and silence encompass him. After taking the highway out of Guthrie, he turned north.

Jim and Carol Hagen lived on a farm at the literal end of the road. He and Pard found their front gate open, almost as if they were expecting them. They pulled to a stop by their front porch and found the couple sitting in the darkness on the porch swing, enjoying the breeze whipped up by the approaching storm. Buck knew, without looking, that they were holding hands.

"Carol said she thought you'd come out tonight," Jim Hagen said.

"Smart woman. Way too smart for you, Sheriff."

Hagen rubbed Pard's head. "You're right. I don't know why she sticks around. Want a beer?"

"He doesn't need a beer," Carol said. "Get him a glass of ice tea."

"Yes dear," Hagen said, disappearing into the house.

Carol was a stunning fifty-something woman. She maintained her girlish figure by riding horses and working the park-like gardens surrounding their modern log cabin. Buck had always thought she was too pretty for Jim Hagen. Looks didn't always matter. Hagen possessed other important things like brains and integrity. Buck sat on the porch, dangling his boots over Carol's purple irises.

"What's the problem?" she asked.

"I got my best friend shot. I'm over thirty and never been married. Hell, I don't even have a steady girlfriend."

"When you're ready to settle down, and you

aren't, you'll find the right woman," she said.

Lightning flashed across the sky, followed by a loud clap of thunder.

"I don't deserve the right woman. Even my best friend can't trust me."

Buck grinned when she said, "Would it make you feel better if I told you no one is perfect?"

"You are."

Carol laughed. "Far from it. I probably aged my poor mother, God rest her soul, by at least twenty years because of my wild ways."

"I'm talking about other things."

"We're talking about the same thing, Buck McDivit. You are feeling guilty because of Trey. Jim said he'll be just fine. You would have done the same for him."

Rain began falling again, this time more than a sprinkle. Buck pulled himself out of the irises and got out of the rain.

"Thanks, Carol. Talking with you always makes me feel better."

She hugged him. "Jim and I are always here for you."

"Did I miss something?" Jim Hagen asked when he returned.

"You know very well you did, you big lug," Carol said. "I'm going to bed. You two have a few things to discuss without me around."

Hagen handed Buck a beer as Carol kissed them both goodnight and departed the front porch.

"Screw the ice tea. I brought Coors. Looks like another storm brewing."

"Now I know why you keep getting elected year after year," Buck said.

"No thanks to you. Pard found Snuffy and the two of them are snuggled up on Snuffy's bed in the kitchen. Why are you so down in the mouth?"

"Is it so apparent?"

"You look like a spanked puppy. Tough

night?"

"It's my cattle rustling investigation. Every time I think I'm getting someplace, I step off into another hole."

The rain had let up, and Buck returned to his perch on the side of the porch. Jim joined him.

"Trey is keeping me abreast of things."

"I'm working on some new information, and this is lots bigger than a renegade cowboy stealing a few head of cattle."

The Hagen's farm lay so far in the woods that you could barely hear semis passing on I-35. Buck remained silent for a moment, listening to night sounds and the wind beginning to whip up.

"I learned something tonight about the operation. Roy Dunlap is doing business with a company called Molasse. Jimmy Quick works both for Roy and for the company as a bodyguard."

"What else?"

"Frankie Boggs, the man murdered on Clayton's farm, was playing around with Dunlap's girlfriend and Dunlap got wind of it."

"Satchel seems to think the murder was passion related. You think Dunlap had Frankie Boggs murdered?"

"Not only that, I think Jimmy Quick is the man who murdered him."

"I'll get us another beer." When Jim returned, thunder rumbled in the distance, the earthy odor of rain-soaked dust saturating the night air.

"Finish your story," he said.

"There's a large and rather sophisticated cattle operation just north of Crescent, not far from the trailer community. Trey and I are sure there are stolen cattle there. He checked into the ownership. It seems untraceable for some reason. It doesn't really matter because it's connected to Dunlap's ranch and the hands apparently work at both places."

Lightning flashed across the sky followed by a nearby clap of thunder. The wind had also kicked up big time, blowing in gusts from the west. Jim gazed up at the sky.

"We have no evidence Quick had anything to do with Boggs' murder."

"Hard to believe. You sure?"

"Satchel wasn't able to turn up a lick of evidence, not even a single clue."

"How can that be possible?"

Hagen shook his head. "I'll look into Molasse for you tomorrow. Have you told anyone else?"

"You're the first to hear about it, boss man."

"I'm not your boss. If I were, I'd have fired you long ago. What about the man stalking the compound?"

"The Lycaia cops took care of the situation," Buck said, not wanting to explain the entire story was concocted.

"You haven't learned anything?"

Jim had no time to quiz him further. With an old flannel robe she wore both winter and summer wrapped tightly around her pajamas, Carol appeared on the porch, a lantern flailing in one hand, Goldie, her orange tabby squirming under her arm. Pard was following them.

"There's a tornado on the ground heading our way."

"Where's Snuffy? Jim asked.

"His bed in the kitchen. I couldn't wake him."

Buck and Pard hurried to the barn, herding the horses and other animals into open pasture. Jim ran into the house to retrieve his dog. It was raining hard when they reached the storm shelter.

"Help me get this thing open," Jim said.

They opened the heavy door, Buck holding it as Jim, Carol and the two dogs hurried down the stairs. The wind had increased in a short time, blowing in ninety-mile-per-hour straight-line gusts as they shut the heavy storm shelter door, securing it with a latch.

"I hate these things," Carol said, sitting on a bench, stroking the nervous cat as she listened to the storm raging outside the shelter between warnings on the weather radio.

Jim had a flashlight and did a quick search for spiders and snakes. Finding none, he sat beside Carol and put his arm around her. Snuffy never missed a beat, curling up beneath their feet and closing his eyes. For the next twenty minutes, they listened as heavy rain, wind and hail pounded the shelter, and watched fitfully as the heavy storm door heaved, trying to fly away into the dark Oklahoma night.

"Nighttime tornadoes are the worst," Jim said, stating a fact all three long-time residents of central Oklahoma already knew.

Rainwater dripped through cracks in the roof, dampening the shelter-seekers, Pard, Carol's tabby and sleeping Snuffy. Finally, the outside cacophony subsided.

The storm had passed, heading east. Buck unlatched the heavy storm door and pushed it open. When they ventured out, what awaited them looked like a scene from a Kafka tale.

Chapter 25

Dime-sized hail, looking like the aftermath of a winter ice storm, covered the ground. Light from the moon behind the clouds reflected off the fallen hail, creating an eerie glow. An oak tree, its trunk shattered and uprooted lay felled not ten feet from the shelter,.

Jim dodged his way through debris strewing the ground as he sprinted toward the house. Buck and Carol found him staring at the roof. As they assessed the damage, the clouds opened to a heavy downpour of warm spring rain. Carol didn't wait, running inside to see what, if anything remained. The roof had a fair-sized hole, mostly over the back of the house. Carol began taping trash bags over the broken windows.

Buck shouted. "You got a tarp or something to cover the hole?"

"In the barn, if we still have one."

Buck sprinted toward it, Jim right behind him. Destructive tornadoes often cut very narrow swaths, leaving some buildings destroyed while the house next door may have no damage at all. They found the barn untouched. Jim quieted the three horses straggling back from the pasture and then climbed into the loft to retrieve a large tarp.

"There's a ladder against the wall, and rope

and bungee cords in the bin over there."

The downpour continued as Buck and Jim climbed up on the roof and situated the tarp over the gaping opening. Water raced down their necks. The high winds had thankfully moved east. Carol met them with towels as they raced into the kitchen.

"There are warm robes in the bathroom," she said. "I've cleaned up the glass and most of the water."

<hr>

They sat at the kitchen table drinking strong coffee when Jim began to laugh. His amusement was contagious. Carol and Buck joined in. When Carol's laughter finally ceased, she started to cry.

"It's all right, baby. No one got hurt, and the horses and other animals are fine. I'll start cleaning this mess up tomorrow."

"I'll help," Buck said.

"No, you won't. You may have damage at your own place you have to clean up."

"Let's hope not," Carol said. "It's after midnight, so you are staying here tonight. We'll get a good night's sleep, and I'll fix us all a country breakfast in the morning. Then we can assess the damage."

"I'm worn out, and so is Pard. You don't have to twist my arm," Buck said.

He'd spent many nights in Jim and Carol's spare bedroom. This particular night, he and Pard were asleep almost as soon as they'd closed their eyes.

<hr>

Buck awoke to the sound of light rain on the windowpane, the appetizing aroma of bacon and eggs wafting from the kitchen. He found Carol and Jim sitting at the table, drinking coffee.

"Good thing we got the tarp up," Jim said. "It rained all night."

"Have much damage inside the house?"

"Nothing we can't dry out. Everything survived except for part of the roof. I have an insurance adjuster on his way to take a look."

"And all the animals are okay," Carol said. "What a blessing."

"Sure I can't help?" Buck asked.

"Get the hell out of here," Jim said.

"I have business I need to attend to before heading home. Can I leave Pard for awhile?"

Pard and his new friend Snuffy were still asleep in Snuffy's bed by the kitchen stove.

"We won't let him starve," Jim said.

<hr>

The sun had come out, three buzzards floating overhead in a blue Oklahoma sky devoid of even a single cloud. Through-the-roof humidity was the only reminder of the previous night's storm. Shutting the windows, Buck turned the air conditioning to high.

He'd headed south on Highway 74 when he noticed a fast approaching vehicle in his rearview mirror. He was doing seventy and guessed the vehicle's speed at ninety. When it neared his rear bumper without trying to pass, he crowded the shoulder of the road.

He was on a long stretch of straight highway with nothing coming in the opposite direction. The driver of the bright blue pickup behind him didn't attempt to pass him, slowing just enough to tuck in less than a few feet away.

Buck took his foot off the gas. When he did, he got a surprise. The truck banged into him hard enough to propel him into the ditch. Fighting the steering wheel, he straightened the path of the Navigator, though only for a moment. The pickup followed him off the road and struck him again.

With barely a moment to glance in his mirror, he saw the blue pickup had a cattle-catcher type bumper extending above its hood. Like a deranged NASCAR driver, the person in the truck began using the bumper to pound the rear of the Navigator.

Buck somehow made it back to the blacktop without crashing.

Realizing the driver of the pickup was deliberately trying to wreck him, he attempted a more radical evasive maneuver, swerving hard left, and then right, hoping to shake the vehicle pasted to his rear end. The person in the truck behind him was obviously an expert driver because nothing Buck did could shake him off his bumper.

The blue pickup banged Buck's vehicle, running him into the ditch again. The Navigator slammed into the deep trench, Buck trying to steer his way out of it until the airbag deployed. When he opened his eyes, he was still in the Navigator, the vehicle lying on its side.

Buck struggled to loosen the seat belt, finally succeeding. He climbed out the smashed window with great difficulty, someone grabbing his arms to help him. In his stupor, he hoped it wasn't the driver of the blue pickup. It wasn't. Four roughnecks, on their way home following their shift on a nearby drilling rig, had eased him out of the truck and laid him in the grass.

"You all right?" one of them asked. "We saw the truck that ran you off the road."

Holding his head, Buck asked, "Did you get his tag number?"

"Couldn't miss it," one of the men with oily faces said. "It was a big Q."

Buck didn't reply, blacking out from the impact of the crash.

⌒⌒⊜⌒⌒

Next time he opened his eyes, a nurse was staring back at him.

"You okay?" she asked.

Buck grabbed the top of his head and winced.

"I think I'm going to throw up."

The nurse whose nametag said Estelle put a pan under his chin and held it there as he vomited into it.

"Sorry," he said as she got rid of the pan and wiped his face with a damp towel.

"Don't worry about it, sweetie," she said. "It's my job."

"What happened?" he asked.

"You're in the emergency room at the Guthrie Hospital. Some roughnecks brought you in. You wrecked your truck."

"Can I go home now?"

"You have a concussion. You'll have to stay until the doctor releases you."

Sheriff Hagen and a Logan County cop hurried into the room.

"Are you okay?" Hagen asked, clutching Buck's hand.

"He'll be fine," the nurse said. "He has a concussion."

"I need to ask him some questions."

Someone entered the room, giving them a start when he walked up behind them and touched Hagen's shoulder.

"Doctor Lee. We need to talk to Buck."

"He's okay, Jim," the man said. "I'll release him tomorrow. Until then, your questions will have to wait. He's in no coherent condition to answer them."

"Make sure he drops by my office," Hagen said as the nurse hustled him and his deputy out the door.

Clayton entered as they exited, his expression beleaguered.

"State troopers called to say my vehicle was in the ditch, the driver taken to the Guthrie Hospital emergency room," he said, ignoring Doctor Lee and Nurse Estelle.

"Sorry about the truck."

"I got plenty of insurance. We're you drunk?"

Clayton turned away from Buck when Doctor Lee answered the question for him.

"Alcohol had no part in the accident. Mr. McDivit's blood-alcohol content was normal. I'm Doctor Lee."

The tall doctor with the gentle voice opened one of Buck's eyelids and stared into his eye as he shined a light into it. Satisfied by what he saw, he patted his shoulder and returned the damp washcloth to his eyes. Clayton was not ready to let the matter drop.

"If he wasn't drunk, why the hell did he run off the road at ten in the morning?"

"Someone ran me into the ditch," Buck said.

"He has a severe concussion. Nothing is broken," Doctor Lee said. "You're upsetting my patient, and you need to leave. He'll answer your questions tomorrow when I release him."

"You tried to put your head through the roof when you hit the ditch," Clayton said. "Why would someone run you off the road?"

Talking was making him nauseous again, and Estelle appeared with the pan and towel. The doctor intervened with Clayton.

"He needs to be on a drip so we can administer acetaminophen. You need to go and let us do our job."

After patting Buck's shoulder, he hurried away to treat another patient. Estelle gave him a dose of something for nausea.

"You heard the doctor. You need to go now," she said.

"Not until he tells me what happened," Clayton said.

Buck held up a palm to stop her when Estelle started to call for assistance.

"Someone in a blue pickup started banging my

rear bumper and ran me into the ditch."

"On purpose?" Clayton said.

Buck cleared his throat. The fluids and pain medicine had yet to start working. Nurse Estelle grabbed his wrist to take his pulse when his eyes rolled back in his head.

"He's in no condition to answer your questions. Please leave now."

Seeing he was going to get no answers, Clayton tipped his hat to Estelle and walked for the door.

"Have him come by my ranch the minute he's released," he said before disappearing down the hallway.

Buck's head felt better when Estelle closed the blinds and turned off the lights. He soon dozed off into a fitful sleep.

Chapter 26

Buck got little rest that night with nurses checking on him every thirty minutes. Whenever he dozed off, they would wake him and stare into his eyes with a small flashlight. Toward dark, he was feeling hungry, and one of the nurses brought him some peach yogurt. His nausea had slowly abated until he was finally able to eat a little food without immediately throwing it up. He didn't know until then he even liked peaches.

Pumped full of fluids, he took many shaky trips to the bathroom, rolling his IV across the floor and not worrying about his bare butt protruding from the back of the hospital gown. At one point, he felt strong enough to look into the closet and found his clothes and cell phone.

His keychain was intact. The jump drive he'd attached to it was missing. When he inspected his aching left shoulder, he saw someone had incised the letter Q into it. It made him realize the big dog fighter's knife had been close enough to his throat to cut it if he had wanted to.

A nurse entered the dark room to check his chart.

"When can I go home?" he asked.

"When the doctor releases you. What you need

now is undisturbed rest."

Buck agreed though wondered why it didn't include the nurses, waking him every time he closed his eyes. When the last nurse had left the room, he dialed Lana.

"Are you okay?"

"I can't recall having a headache like the one I have now. Kristy said you have connections in the business world. I was wondering if you could check on a company for me."

"Kristy already filled me in about your problem. I have my people checking on Molasse Limited, and we'll have an answer for you soon."

"Thanks," he said.

"You're welcome. I don't want the father of my son dying on me before his progeny comes into the world."

Lana signed off before he had a chance to ask her what she meant by the cryptic comment. He slipped the cell phone under his pillow so the nurses wouldn't take it away from him. He soon fell back to sleep.

He needn't have worried about the phone as he got no calls that night. When he awoke, it was morning, and he was staring up into the face of the man with the same pleasant voice as the doctor who had admitted him.

"How do you feel?"

"Like warmed over shit. When can I go home?"

"Right away, and there's someone here to pick you up."

The door opened and Kristy, radiant in a tailored business dress, hugged him. Doctor Lee gave Buck several prescriptions and said farewell. Kristy wheeled him to the elevator, and outside to her Prius.

"Nice ride," he said as she handed him a pair of dark sunglasses.

"They said you might be sensitive to sunlight."

Buck didn't realize how sleepy he was. Soon as he laid his head back against the rest, he fell asleep and didn't awake until Kristy stopped the hybrid in one of Lykaia's underground parking lots.

"Stay put," she said, opening the door and coming around the car to help him. "You are probably still a little shaky."

"More than just a little," he said, light-headed as he climbed from the car.

Kristy made a call on her cell phone, a woman in an electric vehicle soon joining them. She took them to Esme's teepee and dropped him off. Esme was outside, waiting for him. Although he didn't feel helpless, he reveled in Esme's attention as she gave him a hand into the teepee. After laying him on soft bedding, she began removing his clothing.

"I'm not an invalid, you know?"

"Stop bellyaching," she said.

Tucking him beneath the covers, she dabbed his face with an aromatic potion.

"This is soothing, and it has an herbal ingredient which will prevent you from losing consciousness."

"I'll bet it won't keep me from falling asleep. The nurses at the hospital kept me awake all night, and I can't recall ever being this tired."

"You can sleep now without worry. You will awaken fully refreshed."

Buck dozed off shortly after closing his eyes, awakening some twelve hours later, Beauty's tongue licking a warm swath across his face.

"Hey girl," he said, hugging her. "Miss me?"

Beauty had, or else was putting on a good act. She even almost wagged her tail. Esme joined them and rubbed balm on his bruises.

"How do you feel this morning?"

"I don't know what sort of potion you put on my face. You should patent it. I slept like a baby."

Esme had a bowl of something she spoon-fed to him. It tasted like cornmeal and chicken broth, and he felt better after eating it. She also gave him herbal tea that reminded him of the concoction he drank from the old Indian's black cup.

Esme smiled when he finished. "The sleep, poultices, and nourishment will help return your strength. Now, there are things we must discuss."

"Sounds ominous."

"More than you know," she said.

"Then don't keep me in suspense."

"Not here, at a place not far away. Can you walk?"

Buck nodded. "I'm a little shaky on my feet. I think what's causing it is the tea you gave me."

He felt woozy as he pulled the covers away, glancing around for something to wear.

"No need for clothes where we are going."

She took his hand and led him along a path through the forest until they reached what seemed to him the same clearing where he'd met the old Indian. The old man's cabin was gone, though not the tranquil sound of falling water. A small waterfall plunged from the cliff, the pool beneath it so clear and blue he could see every detail of its sandy bottom. Esme stripped away her clothes and led him into the pool.

"Where are we?"

"We have crossed," she said.

The clearing seemed exactly as he remembered it, except with no ground fog or giant butterflies. Esme swam toward the eddy beneath the falling water, and he followed her. Swimming beneath the waterfall, she stopped just inside the mouth of a small grotto and sat on the sandy bottom.

"Where is the old Indian?" he asked.

"Everywhere; he is with us now."

"How is that possible?"

"Close your eyes and count to ten before you open them."

She was gone when he opened his eyes. "Where are you?"

"Beside you," she said, giving him a start.

When he turned, she was sitting on the other side of him.

"Great trick. How'd you do it?"

Her image glimmered and then disappeared as he looked at her. She appeared again in her original position.

"You think I'm tricking you? Maybe I have you drugged and hypnotized. You wouldn't know if I did."

"Am I?"

"No more than normal," she said. "We are sitting in the Pool of Life. Look at your bruises."

Buck glanced at his arms and legs, his bruises gone, the letter Q Jimmy Quick cut into his shoulder now nonexistent."

"This must be a dream," he said.

"Can you tell the difference between a dream and reality?"

He didn't have an answer though the warmth and proximity of her body seemed very real to him. He'd never seen her in the full light of day before. Her dark hair was close to black, her eyes also black, with a luminous purple tinge. Every feminine turn of her body was perfect, and her face caused him to think of a beautiful Mayan maiden, complete with ceremonial tattoo. She smiled when she noticed him staring at her.

"Like what you see?"

"You already know the answer to that question. Why did you bring me here?"

"You are in grave danger. As much as I love you, it is beyond my power to protect you."

"Jimmy Quick?"

"He means to kill you and drag you to hell.

Another spirit has followed him from the Underworld. A shape-shifter and Quick's bitter enemy. He'll take you too if he can."

It was dark when Buck awoke again. This time he felt strong when he stood. The fire in the center of the teepee emitted only faint illumination, though he could see his bruises were gone. He pulled a colorful serape over his shoulders and joined Esme and Beauty outside as they watched a pot simmer over an open fire.

"I thought you were going to sleep all day and through the night," she said. "How do you feel?"

"Wonderful, except for the strange dreams the blow to my head seemed to cause."

Esme smiled, and Beauty strode over to him, demanding a few caresses.

They shared the contents of the cooking pot: a well-seasoned stew that reminded him how hungry he was. Coyotes howled in the distance, their chorus accompanied by a nearby owl and an orchestra of crickets and tree frogs. Fireflies lighted the darkness of the surrounding forest, their ephemeral presence reminding him of a certain spirituality he couldn't quite remember.

"Lana will join us soon," Esme said. "She has some information for you and wants to tell you in person."

Lana and Sara soon arrived at Esme's teepee.

"I can't believe you are up and around. Doctor Lee said the wreck could have killed you."

"You spoke with the doctor?"

"He's an old friend."

The storms had dissipated, at least for the moment, the sky luminous with glowing stars and a golden moon that was almost full.

"Sara and I came for a soak in Esme's hot tub. If you join us, I will tell you what I found out about Molasse Limited."

Before he could answer, they headed for the big wooden tub and began stripping off their clothes. Still unused to soaking naked with three women he doffed his own clothes, sinking up to his neck in hot water. Darkness masked his uneasiness.

"Lee said you left the hospital covered in bruises," Lana said. "Where did they all go so fast?"

"I know a wonderful medicine woman," he said. "Please tell me what you know about Molasse Limited."

"The company owns a fleet of specialized planes used to transport horses to races around the world. British billionaires and Saudi sheiks are just part of their clientele. The business has evolved far beyond transporting race horses."

"How so?"

"Say a Kuwaiti businessman would like a Texas longhorn for his desert retreat. He can get one by contacting Molasse. If a rich Hong Kong merchant desires an African Snow Leopard, it can be had, also for a price."

"Molasse is an international dealer in stolen cattle and exotic animals? I didn't realize that there was a market for such things."

"Some cattle breeds are guarded like national treasures. Ranchers in New Zealand have been known to pay fortunes for exotic breeds rustled from Texas and Oklahoma."

"What kind of money are we talking about here?" he asked.

"Millions of dollars," she said. "Molasse will apparently steal any animal if the price is right. A champion horse that had run in the Kentucky Derby went missing a few years ago. It's now reportedly standing stud at a breeding facility in Dubai."

"How did you learn about this?"

"Our circle of business extends around the

world, and an operation as big as Molasse is hard to keep secret. Once I began asking around, the information started flowing freely."

"Why hasn't someone shut them down?" Buck asked.

"International theft is hard to police. Few organizations have global authority."

"Lana, you're amazing," he said.

Sara grabbed Lana's elbow. "Yes she is, and you need to keep your hands off her if you want to continue as the father of our child."

Buck blinked. "What are you talking about?"

"Hasn't Esme told you yet?"

"Told me what?"

"Lana; she's pregnant, and you are the birthfather."

Chapter 27

Buck lay beneath the covers in the teepee, still thinking about Sara's words as he listened to Esme's soft breathing. Sensing he was looking at her, she finally opened her eyes.

"What's the matter?" she asked.

"Apparently I fathered a child with a woman I don't even remember sleeping with."

"You were performing one of your duties as Fertility Deity."

"A situation I was tricked into performing. Something I would never have done had I not been drugged."

"Lana is ruthless when it comes to achieving her goals," Esme said. "She wasn't going to take no for an answer."

"I can't let her get away with it."

"What do you intend to do about it?"

"Sue for custody," he said.

"Lana is more powerful than you realize. You'll be unsuccessful."

"Then what'll I do?"

"She will raise him here at Lykaia. He will have the best upbringing and finest education possible. He will never want for anything."

"That's not true. I never knew my real dad. It's

haunted me every day of my life."

She touched his cheek. "You are a special man. You deserved knowing the joy of a father and a mother. It won't be the case with your child. He'll have you for the rest of his life, and more mothers than he can handle."

The remainder of the night, Buck lay awake, pondering the situation. Esme snuggled against his shoulders and put her arm around him, massaging his chest. She kissed his neck and then whispered in his ear.

"I know you have doubts about becoming a father. You had no choice in the matter. It was your destiny."

Buck needed some answers. One of his questions was how could a forensic investigator as good as Satchel Pratt not have found a single scrap of evidence while investigating the murder of Frankie Boggs. He and Pard headed for Pratt's farm north of Guthrie to ask him. They found him sitting alone on his front porch swing.

"Damn, brother, are you okay? Something must be up for you to drive all the way out here to see ol' Satchel."

Satchel was relaxing with a glass of vodka, water, and ice. He could have been on his tenth one. You couldn't tell because he never acted drunk.

"Remember Pard? You were the one who named him."

Satchel smiled, grabbed his heart, and said, "Hurt me, brother. Need a beer?"

"You read my mind. I know where they are. Can I get you another drink?"

"You're the mind reader," Satchel said. "Vodka's on the kitchen cabinet. Now don't give me a pussy pour."

Satchel was rubbing Pard's ears when Buck

returned with the vodka and beer and joined him on the swing.

"Nice night."

"You didn't come all the way out here to talk about the weather. What's up?"

"The sheriff told me you didn't find a single usable clue in the Frankie Boggs murder."

"Nope, not one."

"How is it possible?"

"I've asked myself the same question a dozen times. It's not possible, or is it?"

Buck told him about Esme's two spirits from hell. "Do you believe in the supernatural?"

Satchel looked at him as if he were crazy. "Hell no; neither do you. Sounds like you were messed up on some hallucinogenic drug."

"But it would explain the lack of clues."

"Hell, brother, you might as well say a magician made the clues disappear. Makes about as much sense and you know damn well it isn't the way things shake out."

Maybe he had been on hallucinogenic drugs. After his visit with the old Indian and his dip in the magic pool with Esme, he wasn't sure what he believed anymore. He'd wracked his brain for other possible explanations and had found none.

"I know the murderer killed Boggs with a knife and carved him up. Did you find any other non-lethal knife wounds on the body?"

"Like what?"

Satchel smiled when Buck said, "Like the letter Q?"

"Whoever killed Boggs carved the letter Q into his back. How did you know?"

"Trey had the same letter carved in his back after the incident at the Rock Bar. Someone cut the same letter on my shoulder after running me off the road and almost killing me. I'm convinced the person responsible for all three acts is Jimmy

Quick."

"Let me see the mark on your shoulder."

"It's gone."

"What do you mean it's gone?"

Buck grinned. "I know you don't believe in the supernatural. Esme washed it away for me in the Pool of Life."

"I know it can't be the beer that's fried your brain. Exactly what are you smoking?"

He didn't wait for an answer, heading for the kitchen and returning shortly with vodka for himself and another Coors for Buck.

"I didn't think I'd had that much to drink. Now, I'm either hammered or else you're full of shit."

"Neither one," Buck said. "Jimmy Quick isn't my biggest problem."

"Then maybe you better tell me what it is because ol' Satchel here is sorta confused."

"Welcome to the club. There was a woman I was going to fix you up with. Now, I think she may be in on the con."

Buck told him the story of breaking into Roy Dunlap's office.

"Georgia was the only person who knew I was in Dunlap's office. Someone tipped off Jimmy Quick. How else would he have known to take the jump drive off my key chain?"

"If you didn't tell her you had taken the information on the jump drive, there's no way she could have known. You said Dunlap is a security freak. If so, he probably has an infrared spy camera in his office. You're lucky the cops didn't bust down the door and cart you off to jail."

Satchel's words made sense.

"Trey and I checked out a little community north of Crescent populated by bikers, meth cookers, and general throwbacks."

"Hell, brother, you wouldn't find a single honest person if you busted the whole place.

That's why I keep an automatic weapon under the bed."

"Yeah, well we found something even more interesting when we drove past it: a holding pen big enough for a hundred head of cattle. We bluffed the guard and Trey got some blood samples. It's a good bet the cows are stolen property. Doesn't matter. The evidence was obtained illegally and is inadmissible in court."

"Did you check out the ownership of the holding pen?"

"An Australian company named Molasse Limited. Roy Dunlap is involved up to his neck. The only problem is we have no real proof."

"You are pretty sure you know where they are taking the stolen cattle. Just get the place busted. You'll find the answers."

"How do I accomplish that little feat without any evidence to get a warrant?"

"Do what all good criminal detectives do when they reach a dead end."

"Maybe you better tell me what that is," Buck said.

"Pick your best suspect, concoct a story the authorities can buy into, lie with a straight face, and then stick to it."

"What happens if we raid the place and find out it's a legitimate operation?"

"You're young, and Mexico's not so far away. You might even find yourself a pretty senorita down there that you really like."

Chapter 28

Two days had passed before Buck and Pard visited Clayton's ranch to check in. After thinking about Satchel's advice, he'd decided deception was the only way he was ever going to crack this case. After sleeping on it, he'd devised a plan.

Satchel's words about Mexico kept echoing in his head as he patted Pard and told him to wait outside the house. If he were wrong about the cattle holding facility, he would have hell to pay. He thought about it as he climbed the steps to Clayton's veranda.

"Where in the hell have you been?" Clayton asked.

"I wasn't feeling well so I just sort of crashed out for a few days. I'm ready to get back to work now."

"Glad to hear it. You totaled the Navigator, so a new one's waiting for you in the parking lot."

"You didn't have to do that."

"I don't have to do anything. Wait here while I go find Maria."

When Clayton went down the hall, KK appeared from behind their bedroom curtain wearing little more than a sheer pink wisp of a baby doll nightgown. In tears, she hurried across the veranda and hugged him.

"Why didn't you call?" Buck had no good answer for her and cringed when she said, "I have something to tell you."

"Not something to do with our last night together, I hope."

KK's tears continued flowing freely. "Yes, it does."

"What?" he asked.

"I know you love me. I love you too, but we have no future together. Clayton is my man, so please don't tell him about the other night."

"You have my word on it," he said.

KK was gone when Clayton returned. "I called the sheriff. He's on his way over. We have some talking to do."

Clayton relaxed in his serape-draped rocking chair and waited until Maria brought whiskey for him and coffee for Buck. Sheriff Hagen had arrived before he needed a refill.

"Where in the hell have you been?" he asked. "You were supposed to come by the office and fill me in on what happened to you."

"I was sort of whacked when I left the hospital. I've been pretty much out of it for the last few days."

"Carol and I've been worried sick," he said."

"I know. I'm sorry. I kind of lost track of time. I'm fine now."

"I've already given Buck a ration of shit," Clayton said. "Now, we got other things to talk about."

"Tell me about the wreck," Hagen said.

"Someone in a blue pickup with a cattle catcher bumper ran me off the road. Though I couldn't see the driver's face, for my money it was Jimmy Quick."

"What reason did he have to run you off the road?" Hagen asked.

"I had something he wanted."

"Such as?"

"A jump drive containing some damning information. He took the jump drive from my keychain. Doesn't matter because I'd already printed the file."

Opening a Manila folder, he showed them the contents.

"Buck seems to think it's valuable information," Clayton said.

"I'm listening."

"I told you about the cattle operation north of Crescent. Trey and I both believed it's where the rustlers are taking stolen cows. Well, now I have proof."

Buck handed a sheet of paper to the sheriff as Clayton craned to have a look.

"What is it?"

"A document linking Roy Dunlap to cattle rustling, and oil theft from Crescent Oil."

Sheriff Hagen frowned after taking a quick look.

"How did the person that ran you off the road know you had a jump drive with this information on it?" Hagen asked.

"Roy was at the horse races in Hot Springs when I broke into his office. He's a security freak, by all accounts and probably has an infrared camera recording everything that goes on in his office."

"And?" Hagen said.

"Jimmy Quick works for him. When Roy realized I'd compromised his computer, he had Quick chase me down to retrieve the jump drive."

"This is pretty damning evidence. Still, it's tainted and you know we can't use it."

"Bullshit!" Clayton said. "You're telling me we know who is stealing my cows, and my oil, and we can't do anything about it?"

"This document won't stand up in court."

"It's reason enough to get a warrant to search Roy's ranch," Buck said.

"We need something other than this. No judge would issue a warrant, considering the way the information was obtained."

"To hell with that!" Clayton said. "I play poker and golf with practically every judge around. I'll get one to sign it tonight if need be."

Sheriff Hagen didn't seem convinced. "You sure about this, Buck? It's my ass if we bust this place in error."

"Sheriff, I'm positive this cattle facility is involved in the cattle theft rampant around here."

"Well, it's settled then," Clayton said, punching in a number on his cell phone. "I'm calling Judge Mannock right now. You get a warrant ready. I'll get it signed."

"I think we are moving way too fast," Sheriff Hagen said.

"We are," Buck said. "I haven't told you everything I know."

"Then tell us now," Clayton said.

"The Lykaia compound has contacts all over the world. Lana checked on Molasse Limited for me."

"The head lady at Lycaia?" Sheriff Hagen asked.

"Yes."

"She would know," Hagen said. "That woman is connected to people all over the world. What did she say about the company?"

"They deal in valuable stolen livestock such as race horses, exotic animals, and rare breeds of cattle."

Clayton was suddenly interested. "They don't sell them at your local cattle barn?"

"Hardly," Buck said. "More like to rich breeders, emirs, and corporate CEO's, and anywhere in the world from Dubai to New Zealand. According to Lana, Roy and Jimmy Quick work indirectly for Molasse."

"This operation extends far outside my jurisdiction," Hagen said. "We need to get some other agencies involved before we jump off the deep end on this."

"Agreed," Clayton said. "However this thing shakes out, I intend to be involved."

Chapter 29

Buck sat on the front porch with Carol and Jim. Well after dark, Jim and Buck were drinking beer. Carol sipped iced tea as he tried to explain why he hadn't called them immediately after the hospital released him.

"I'm sorry. I had business I needed to attend to first."

Carol wasn't buying it. "I have known you since you were a snotty-nosed teenager. What was so important you couldn't have called and told me you were okay?"

"It's sort of complicated."

"No it isn't, you just don't want to tell me."

"Because I think it's something you don't want to hear."

"Don't you trust me enough to tell me anyway?"

Jim Hagen was staying out of the argument, pacing the porch as he drank his beer. Still, he missed none of the conversation.

Buck said, "You know I trust you."

"You are making me mad. You tell me now, Buck McDivit, and don't leave anything out."

Jim Hagen winced when Buck said, "I told you

I had sex with a woman and now she's pregnant."

"Are you in love with this woman?" Carol asked.

"I hardly know her. I don't even remember having sex with her."

"Then how do you know you did?" Jim asked.

"She told me."

"And you believe her?"

"It's Lana," Buck said.

"From Lycaia?" Jim asked.

"Who is Lana?" Carol asked.

"One of the most politically and financially powerful persons in Oklahoma."

"And you don't remember having sex with her?" Carol asked.

Jim chimed in. "You got the head honcho of Lycaia pregnant, and you don't even remember having sex with her?"

"Drugs were involved."

"What kind of drugs, and since when did you start using drugs?" Carol asked.

"They were Indian medicine drugs I took unwittingly during an ancient religious ceremony."

It was Carol's turn for her eyes to grow large. "An ancient religious ceremony?"

"Maybe more like a pagan revel."

"Have you flipped totally out?" Jim said with a growl.

"Something compromised my defenses."

"Like what?"

"A hundred or so gorgeous naked women."

Having no basis to comment, Jim and Carol simply stared at him in stunned disbelief.

"This is getting stranger by the minute," Carol finally said. "Maybe you better explain."

Buck told them about the spring solstice ceremony, leaving nothing out, except the parts he couldn't remember.

"Their religious tradition dictated I have sex

with the secular head of Lykaia. I returned the next night because I thought I was working on an investigation. Whatever they put in my drink caused me to become sexually potent, which makes me glad their tradition stopped at one."

Following a derisive laugh, Jim asked, "So none of this is your fault?"

"Hell, how can you father a child and not be at fault? I'm not proud of what I did, and I take full responsibility."

Carol grabbed his hand. "Do the grandparents have any privileges?"

Buck smiled. "I would hope so. They may be pagans. They aren't barbarians."

Having told Carol and Jim, the closest thing to parents he ever had, about his impending child lifted a huge weight off his shoulders. He wasn't prepared for Carol's reaction when Jim dropped another bomb on her.

"Buck and I have something else to tell you."

"As important as what I just heard?"

Jim nodded. "Different though just as important."

"Then I think you should wait a minute before you tell me," she said, leaving them and going to the house. She returned with a bottle of Weller's and three tumblers filled with ice. "Bottoms up," she said after pouring each of them a liberal portion of whiskey. "Now tell me what's so important."

Jim explained as briefly as possible about the illegal cattle operation. "We are going to bust the perps. Buck has asked to be involved, and I have given my approval."

"Involved? What exactly do you mean?"

"I'm going to be part of the SWAT team."

"I see," she said. "First you tell me I'm about to have the grandchild I've prayed for all my life, and now you say their father may not be around to enjoy the baby with me?"

Buck shook his head. "It's not so dangerous,"

"Jim, how dangerous is this operation?"

"Maybe you better give me more Weller's," he said.

Carol poured them all a fresh shot and then said, "Well?"

"It could be dangerous. We'll have the advantage of surprise. We should have everything under control before a shot is fired."

Carol's mouth opened wide. "How many men are involved?"

"I don't know, a hundred maybe."

"Good God, Jim! A hundred men?

"There's lots of ground to cover."

She stared at Buck and said, "Not dangerous?"

"I was on the SWAT team when I was a cop in Oklahoma City. I took part in a couple dozen assaults. I never got hurt."

Carol started to cry. "You got shot in the stomach once."

"Barely. A ricochet caught the bottom of my bulletproof vest. The bullet hardly penetrated the skin."

Carol slugged her shot of Weller's, poured herself another, and then drained it. Hurrying to the front door, she turned before entering. Tears streamed from her eyes as she pointed at Buck.

"Don't you dare get yourself killed and prevent me from seeing the only grandchild I'll probably ever have."

Buck and Jim watched her disappear into the house. Not bothering to pour himself a fresh shot of whiskey, he drank straight from the bottle and then handed it to Buck.

Buck took his own healthy swig. "You okay?"

"I'm fine. It's just we've been married close to thirty years. I've been in mortal danger because of my job more times than I can count and Carol has never once cried because of it.”

Buck tapped his shoulder. “She wasn't crying because of me either. She was thinking about her future grandbaby.”

Chapter 30

Buck spent much of the next day worrying about his impending fatherhood. He worked in the barn, playing with Pard, grooming the horses and getting in Hector's way until the little man with dark hair and big smile grabbed his elbow.

"Want to tell me what's wrong?"

"What makes you think something's wrong?"

"Because you are following me around like a sick colt. Now, either go away and leave me alone or tell me your problem."

Hector smiled when Buck said, "I'm going to be a father."

"Wonderful." The smile disappeared from his face, and he said, "But you are not married, are you?"

Buck shook his head. "Not even close."

Hector led him to a chair in the barn, sat him down, and then stood in front of him in a lecturing posture. Buck realized what he was about to hear would not be complimentary.

"Did you get a girl pregnant accidentally?"

"I wasn't really thinking about it if that's what you mean."

Hector shook his head and frowned, revealing

the gap in his front teeth. "You have to make this right. What you did is a sin. You have to marry the girl."

Hector's dark eyes grew even larger when Buck said, "I think she's already married."

When Buck explained, Hector became very agitated and began talking in Spanish. He yelled for LaDona who came running out of the house to check on the commotion. After a lengthy and animated conversation in Spanish, the two turned to Buck, glaring at him.

"You must consult our priest," she said. "He'll know what to do."

Buck seriously doubted he would, especially once he told him the mother-to-be was a practicing member of the Southern Death Cult religion. He decided to withhold that tidbit of information from Hector and LaDona, as they were already upset. He finally promised them he would speak with Father Sanchez. The pledge failed to assuage his feelings though earned him supportive smiles from the couple.

What Buck needed, he realized, was a healing ride on his pony. Lady was more than ready for him, snorting and moving her head as he saddled and bridled her. The ride was what they both needed and two hours had passed when they trotted back to the barn, Pard wagging his tail as he followed along behind.

They found Kristy's Prius parked in front of the barn. She was sitting on the porch with Hector and LaDona. They were all laughing, LaDona hugging her. She had obviously made a good impression on the couple because Hector pumped his hand.

"Kristy is a wonderful woman. You are a lucky man."

Glancing at Kristy, he said, "I have to hose Lady down and settle her."

"Take your time. We're having a nice visit."

Buck was brushing Lady's mane when Kristy joined him in the stall. Lady and Pard took to her immediately.

"Hector and LaDona think I'm having your baby," she said.

"Sorry for the confusion. I made the mistake of telling them that I'm going to be a father. When you showed up, they just naturally connected the dots."

"You didn't try to correct them," she said.

"Sorry about that."

"It's okay," Kristy said, rubbing Lady's head. "She is such a beautiful animal. I've never touched a horse before now."

"You have to be kidding. You grew up in Oklahoma and have never touched a horse?"

"I grew up in Texas. I don't know why; I just never had the opportunity to ride a horse."

It was Buck's turn to smile. "I think I can arrange it. Is everything okay?" he asked, again wondering about the purpose of her visit.

"Lana sent me to check on you."

"For what reason?"

"Like you said, you're going to be the father of her child. She wanted me to check out where you live and who you associate with."

"To make sure I'm not an unfit father?"

"Something like that," she said.

"Come upstairs. I'll give you a look at where I live."

Buck gave her a quick tour of his apartment, pointing out the Oriental rugs, wood floors and demonstrating the gold-plated faucets.

"Ooh, this is wonderful. I didn't realize you were so wealthy."

"I'm not. My landlady is. I help out around the place in exchange for free board for Lady, Pard and me."

"What kind of help?" Kristy asked.

"Mostly lending Hector a helping hand at feeding and caring for the horses."

"Looks to me like he does most of the work," she said.

"You're right. I fell into a bird's nest on the ground when she hired me for this gig. I'm definitely not complaining."

"I wouldn't think so," she said.

"Does your visit mean Lana's considering letting my son spend time with me?"

"I think it's more of the other way around."

"Oh?"

"Though she didn't come out and tell me this, I think she's looking for a way to keep you from seeing the boy."

"That's what I was afraid of," he said. "What should I do about it?"

Kristy touched the back of his hand. "I'll give her my best recommendation. So will Esme. Lana will come around."

"Are you sure?"

"I've been her personal assistant for five years. She's a tough businesswoman but has a heart of gold."

Hector and LaDona waved as Kristy drove away in her electric-powered car.

"You're a lucky man," LaDona said.

"I hope so," Buck said.

Chapter 31

"What's taking so long?" Clayton O'Meara asked as he paced around the table.

"Knock it off, Clay. You aren't even supposed to be here, remember?" Sheriff Hagen said.

The windowless room was abuzz with activity, television screens and computer monitors flickering as several uniformed operators entered data from their keyboards. Five men, including Sheriff Hagen, sat around a conference table strewn with maps and activity reports. Two of the men wore suits marking them as O.S.B.I.

"This place gives me the creeps. It reminds me of something out of the Cold War."

"Quit belly-aching, O'Meara. There are some of us here that actually participated in the Cold War."

Agent Gray Norman's words caused Clayton to frown and glance at his watch again. Taller and older than Clayton, Norman's expensive suit and well-coiffed white hair marked him as someone near the pinnacle of the Bureau's hierarchy. His younger partner seemed unimpressed by his stature.

"Twenty minutes and counting," the younger

man said as he glanced at the television screen.

Harold Taylor's cheap suit marked him as a junior agent though his height was no less impressive than Norman's was. His shoulders were as wide as a tight end for the Dallas Cowboys.

"Lance Jameson's limo is pulling into the compound grounds."

Clayton asked, "Who is he and what's his importance?"

"From what we know, he's the head man at Molasse. He rarely leaves Australia, so this must be an important visit. There's a big party going on to impress him."

Sheriff Hagen fidgeted with a pencil. "He keeps a low profile. His entire dossier is no more than a page long."

Clayton glared at Gray Norman. "What are we paying you people for if you can't even amass vital information?"

"I don't like your attitude, O'Meara."

"Yeah, well what are you going to do about it?"

"Maybe I'll kick your ass."

"You and what army?"

"I don't need an army, and I think you have an overblown opinion of yourself."

Captain Dave Warren, the Logan County second-in-command, interrupted the two squabbling men.

"Gentlemen, we are about to go live. I suggest you settle your differences later unless you want them aired across Oklahoma."

Gray Norman returned to his chair, as did Clayton.

Several TV screens suddenly came alive, focusing on police and plain-clothes cops occupying similar rooms, somewhere in other counties.

"Same here in Seminole County."

"Lincoln County is ready."

"Ditto, Cleveland."

The camera focused on Sheriff Hagen. "I'm Jim Hagen, Sheriff of Logan County. Our SWAT team is in place outside the compound north of Crescent. There's a delay. We are on hold for Operation Race Horse to begin.

Someone from another county was getting antsy. "What's the delay?"

"A tall fence surrounds the compound. There's a guard at the gate. From our surveillance, we've learned the operation's supervisor, driving an armored Hummer, reports to the compound every night around ten. He's running late, probably because of the party in progress."

"What's the significance of the Hummer?"

"Our team is in hiding across the road. They plan to follow the vehicle into the compound once the guard opens the gate."

Can't they just climb the fence?"

'We think the gate and fence have sensors that would send an alarm to the house and spoil our surprise."

"Then what do we do?"

"Wait."

⌁

A SWAT team comprised of police officers from Logan and Oklahoma Counties waited across from the gated compound, a lavish party in full swing at the house on the hill. The team had hiked through the woods, cross-country to their present location. The single road leading to the compound had remained guarded since Buck and Trey's visit.

Thirty men dressed in camouflage fatigues and dark hoods sprawled on their stomachs, waiting for the arrival of a black Hummer. A horsefly buzzed around Buck's head as sweat trickled down his face. The cross-country trek had tired him, making his bulletproof vest feel extra constricting.

He had removed the backpack he'd used to carry water and extra ammunition on their trek. Once the attack began, he would no longer need it. Another half-hour had passed before they heard the rumbling of the heavy Hummer coming down the road. Every man along the row grew ready.

When the guard recognized the black vehicle, the heavy gate began opening slowly. As it did, a SWAT team sharpshooter ran behind the Hummer. When the dark vehicle headed up the landscaped pathway to the large house on the hill, the sniper dispatched the guard with a single tranquilizer dart to his neck.

The sergeant in command said, "Move out, single file."

Buck waited until the man in front of him entered the open gate of the compound before following him across the rural road. Headphones connected the team, although they needed little prompting to carry out the well-rehearsed operation. The SWAT unit moved toward the mansion by way of advancing shadows. Within minutes, they had the large structure cordoned. Still undetected, they awaited orders.

The noisy party, along with many guests moving in and out of the house, compromised the guards at the doors. Fifty or more boisterous visitors carried on outside by the pool. A band played, and drinks flowed liberally. Another fifty police officers awaited word the assault had begun. Disguised as church members in buses, they turned off Highway 74, onto the road to the compound moments after the first wave compromised the front gate.

Sharpshooters soon identified their targets. When the lead sergeant gave the command, they took out their respective targets with tranquilizer darts and began advancing on the mansion. Buck was among the first to enter the building and found a raucous party in progress. A collision with a security guard jarred his headphone loose, knocking it across the floor.

The orchestra, security guards, and partiers grew quiet when the SWAT team appeared, automatic weapons drawn and ready. Buck loosened himself from the stunned security guard when he saw someone coming down the stairs he recognized. The sight of her almost caused him to stop dead in his tracks. It was Georgia.

Chapter 32

From the way she clutched the banister, Georgia was apparently quite dazed. Tears streaked her makeup, her hair a mess. Someone had ripped the front of her pink party gown. She also had black eyes and swollen lips. Although she clutched the torn bodice, her efforts did little to hide the gown grown red with blood. Buck's dark mask frightened her, and she backed against the banister.

"It's me," he said, uncovering his face to show her who he was. "Are you okay?"

"This isn't my blood if that's what you mean," she said, hugging him.

"You have to find a place to hide, or you'll be arrested."

"I can't go back upstairs. Roy will kill me."

"Is he alone?"

"He's with Jimmy Quick and a man with an Australian accent. They tried to force me to have sex with them. I stabbed the Aussie in the leg with a ceremonial dagger Roy keeps on his desk as a letter opener. I must have struck a vein or artery because blood began gushing everywhere."

Buck glanced around, looking for someone to help him, wondering if he had time to go downstairs and call for backup.

"Is there another way out of the house?"

Georgia nodded. "A secret passage. I saw Roy use it once. He bloodied my lip and told me to forget about what I'd seen if I knew what was good for me."

"Take me to it," he said.

Shouts from SWAT team members, along with general chaos, confusion, and vocal protests of arrested guests died away as they hurried upstairs, finding Roy's office door ajar. The lavishly decorated room was empty.

Georgia pointed. "The passage is behind that panel. I don't know how to open it."

Buck began feeling the wall, hoping to find the opening mechanism. Finally, he kicked a hole in it with his boot and crawled through.

"Wait for me," Georgia said.

"Too dangerous. Stay here."

"No way," she said, following him through the hole, into the darkness.

Buck groped for a light switch. Finding none, he began descending a circular staircase, Georgia clutching the back of his shirt. Within minutes, they saw a light up ahead. It was a small fluorescent bulb above a closed door.

"On the ground," he said.

Finding the door locked, Buck blasted it with his assault rifle. When he kicked it open, he stared into the startled eyes of Jimmy Quick. Before he could react, Quick unloaded his 9 mm Glock, bullets wheeling him around. Losing his footing, he fell backward, onto the cement floor. Quick was on him in an instant, ripping off his black mask.

"You asshole! I should have known it was you."

Quick pointed the pistol between Buck's eyes. For a moment, he thought he was a dead man. Quick had other ideas.

"A bullet through the brain is too easy for you. This won't be our last meeting. Next time I'll take my time and make you wish I'd already killed you."

Instead of shooting him, Quick kicked Buck in the head and then hurried away down the darkened hallway. Dazed, he lay in a stupor until a crying Georgia lifted his head and rubbed his cheek.

"Oh my God, Buck! Please don't be dead."

He shook the cobwebs from his head and prodded the tender spots beneath the bulletproof vest with his fingers.

"My vest saved me. Help me up."

Georgia's tears grew heavier as she pulled him into a sitting position. He winced, fearing broken ribs when she hugged him.

"Let's get out of here," she said.

Georgia turned and took a step toward the spot where Buck had first seen Jimmy Quick.

"Wait!" he yelled as an explosion rocked the darkness behind them.

Quick had armed a booby trap, destroying a large part of the secret passageway. Acrid smoke began filling the narrow hall as Buck realized there was now only one way out.

Buck's ribs hurt like hell, though a steady surge of adrenaline into his bloodstream got him moving again. Unbuttoning his camouflage shirt, he removed his bulletproof vest, handing Georgia the shirt. She put it on, and they started forward at a rapid clip.

"I can't wait on you," he finally said.

"I run 10 K's. You'll probably have trouble keeping up with me."

"Then let's do it," he said, sprinting down the dimly lit hallway.

Her pink party dress in shambles, Georgia matched Buck stride for stride. When they reached the end of the tunnel, they heard the throaty roar of a revving airplane engine. Pushing open a heavy door, they watched as Jimmy Quick's blue pickup truck kicked up a plume of dust and disappeared down a dirt road.

The tunnel had led them to a spot some distance from the compound. A short dirt runway extended from a hanger, hidden from above by camouflaged netting. A red windsock was the only indication the dusty area was anything more than a horse pasture.

A very small two-seater plane had taxied to the other end of the runway, apparently to take advantage of a steady wind. Realizing it was Roy and Lance making their escape, Buck dropped to a prone position on the runway, pointed his H & K MP5 assault rifle at the plane's engine block, and opened fire. Three well-placed bullets found a cylinder, causing the engine to seize. The plane was moving fast. Even though it would never leave the ground, it continued rushing toward him.

Buck emptied the rest of the thirty-round clip into the wheels and struts. As if in slow motion, the little plane nosed into the ground and skidded to a halt, coating him with oil, dirt, and smoke. One of the plane's doors opened, and Roy Dunlap rolled out, raising his arms when he saw the weapon pointed at him. Intent on the wounded Australian in the smoking plane, Buck popped in another clip and then handed the MP5 to Georgia.

"Kill him if he makes a move."

Georgia looked a mess, her hair beyond mussed and her party dress in tatters. With her finger on the trigger, she pointed the assault weapon at Dunlap, her angry stare daring him to move. Buck ran to the passenger side of the plane, forced open the door and pulled the injured Lance Jameson to safety.

Either Dunlap or Quick had tied a tourniquet around Jameson's thigh. It had probably kept him from bleeding to death. He looked in poor shape when Buck pulled him away from the smoking plane and laid him on the ground.

He didn't have to wonder how they would get the injured man back to the compound as a half dozen SWAT team members soon joined them. An ambulance also arrived, along with a police cruiser. They returned Georgia and him to the grounds of the compound where the operation was mopping up, loading people into buses with barred windows. One of the deputies grabbed Georgia's elbow and directed her to get in line. Buck gave the man a shove, facing him when he wheeled around.

"She's not going to County with the others."

The man had already worked himself into a serious state of anger, his frowning face visibly red, even in dim moonlight.

He was spitting when he said, "Our orders are to bring everyone in, and that means in the bus."

"No way. She's a material witness. Her life wouldn't be worth a plug nickel."

The man's nametag said Deputy Brewster, Oklahoma County. He had the build of a weightlifter and the shaved head of a person who took his job in law enforcement seriously. With his hand on his service revolver, he got into Buck's face.

"You're overstepping your authority. You're not even a real cop."

Buck showed him his badge. "Not only am I sworn in, but I'm also a Logan County deputy. In case you forgot, we're in Logan and not Oklahoma County. Now take your hands off the woman."

"You want a piece of my ass, I'll be happy to oblige you," the Oklahoma County deputy said, edging closer to Buck's face.

By now, a crowd had gathered, forming a circle around the two men. It was then the officer in charge stepped forward. Sergeant Lawson was as young as Buck and bigger than Brewster. Unlike Brewster, his own dark eyes were introspective and not angry. One of Sheriff Hagen's key men, he knew Buck and was aware of his relationship with the sheriff.

"What's going on here?" he said, stepping between Buck and Brewster.

"This woman is a key witness in this case. She will be in mortal danger if she gets on the bus with everyone else."

"We have officers watching the situation. She goes on the bus."

Buck popped the clip into his MP5 and took a step backward. "Over my dead body."

"You want to die because of this woman?" Sergeant Lawson asked.

"Do you?"

Seeing things were out of hand, Lawson glanced at the armed officers behind him, raised his hand, and shook his head.

"Just be cool. I'm calling Sheriff Hagen."

Explaining the situation to the sheriff, he cautiously handed the cell phone to Buck.

"What in the cornbread hell is going on out there? Put the woman on the bus and get your ass in here. Now!"

"No can do, sheriff."

"That's the procedure, and you need to follow it. Put your weapon down."

"Let me talk to Clayton."

Thinking he had diffused the standoff, he handed the phone to Clayton.

"I have Georgia with me. She stabbed the Australian when he and Jimmy Quick tried to rape her. She'll be in danger, maybe even killed if she gets in one of those buses."

"Hold the phone," he said, turning to Sheriff Hagen, and Agents Norman and Taylor. "Gentlemen, the woman Buck is protecting is an employee of mine. McDivit is also my employee, and he believes she would be in grave danger if she gets on one of the buses. I think so too."

"What do you suggest we do then, O'Meara?" Agent Norman asked.

"The President and the last three Presidents are all personal friends of mine. I'm not suggesting anything, I'm telling you. If one hair on the woman's head is harmed, or Buck McDivit's, I'm going to personally see to it everyone in this room is busted back to the same rank they were the day they started. Now, someone had better make a quick and sane decision here, or I'm going to start making phone calls."

Clayton returned the phone to Sheriff Hagen, walked across the room and poured a cup of coffee.

"Put Sergeant Lawson back on the line."

"Yes sir," Lawson said.

"Get the buses moving. You stay with Buck and the woman until I get there."

"But . . ."

"You have your orders, Sergeant. They require no explanation. Are you clear on this?"

Lawson had no time to reply because Sheriff Hagen had hung up the phone.

Chapter 33

Buck lay in Esme's teepee, trying not to grimace as the gorgeous woman administered a poultice to the three purple bruises coloring his chest. Beauty licked his hand, and he stroked her long muzzle.

"You are beginning to perturb me, Buck McDivit. I've only known you a short while, and I've already lost count of the times you've needed critical care."

She frowned and shook her head when he said, "I usually go a year or more between major wounds."

"Not funny. I'm worried about Quick. He's tried to kill you three times already. Next time you may not be so lucky."

"He's probably in Mexico by now. If he is still in Logan County, the sheriff will track him down. Too many people know him."

"I might have believed it a week ago. Now, I'm not so sure. Will you stay with me tonight?"

"I can't though there's no place I'd rather be. I have a meeting with Sheriff Hagen and the O.S.B.I. first thing tomorrow."

"You could leave from here. I'll get you up."

"My notes are back at Sunset Farms. Trey is picking me up at six."

Esme rustled through a small cabinet, returning with a necklace bearing a gold pendant of the same rattlesnake image as the tattoo on her shoulder. Putting it around his neck, she fastened the clasp.

"You must promise me you won't take this off."

"What is it?"

"A powerful talisman. Nothing can protect you if the Great Spirit deems it so, though this will ward off most evil spirits. Promise me you won't remove it."

"The authorities will think I'm crazy."

"Promise me."

Buck bent forward and kissed her. "Evil spirits will have to rip it from my dying body."

Esme squeezed his hand. "Don't joke about things like this. I would feel lots better if you took Beauty with you."

"I can't take her to the meeting. I'll be fine, I promise."

When Esme kissed him, tears filled her eyes. "I must take a journey, and I may never see you again."

"Where are you going?"

"As I told you, I'm a traveler through time. Soon, Princess and I must return to our real home."

"Where is this place?"

"In distance, it's not far from here. In time, it's a thousand years away."

"What's it like?"

"Like no other place on earth," she said. "My city occupies a hill overlooking a bend in a mighty river. A palisade surrounds the city, and I live in a regal pyramid."

"Sounds wonderful. I'd love to visit sometime," he said. "Is it possible?"

"I can't be sure if I'll ever see you again once I

go. If our destinies determine that we will, then I'll send you a message."

"How will I know it's from you?"

"You will know."

Buck took her hand and kissed it, and then knelt beside Princess and hugged her beautiful neck.

She didn't answer him, saying something in an unfamiliar language as she waited by the flap of the teepee.

"The sound of danger is singing in my brain. I can't make it stop. Go now. Sleep with an ear to the ground and one eye open."

Buck's new Navigator waited at Lykaia's front gate where Kristy dropped him off.

"You be careful, Buck McDivit."

"Stop it. Esme has me spooked enough as it is."

"Because she loves you."

"And I love her. I'll be fine."

The sky was dark as he exited the commune and entered the thick covering of trees leading back to the nearest section line road. He had traveled less than a tenth of a mile when a blue pickup burst from the darkness and nailed into the Navigator's right front fender, powering it into the ditch. Jimmy Quick was on him as he opened the door, tossing a noose around his neck and yanking.

Buck rolled out of the cab, onto the ground, as Quick pulled hard on the rope. Struggling to catch his breath, he caught the hilt of Quick's heavy hunting knife across his temple. It was the last thing he remembered for a while.

Chapter 34

Buck's head throbbed when he opened his eyes and found he was naked, lying on his back in damp sand. A man stood over him. He could clearly see in the dim fluorescence of a camping lantern that it was Jimmy Quick. When he tried to rise, he realized heavy wire bound his hands behind his back. A knife cut oozing blood extended from his breastbone to just below his belly button.

"You are about to die, McDivit. First, I'm going to make you beg me to kill you."

Buck's blood had already attracted mosquitoes and horseflies. They flittered in and out of his wound. Unable to swat them away, he tried to ignore them, knowing he had much deeper concerns to worry about.

"In case you think someone might come to your rescue before I kill you, better think again. Your Lincoln is in the creek, out of sight from the road. They won't find your bones until next spring."

Seeing the magic talisman around Buck's neck, Quick yanked it, breaking the string, and dropping it into the sand.

"Nice try. Someone very powerful is watching out for you. They'll be upset when they find your rotting body."

Buck struggled to free his hands bound with baling wire. His feet were free, and when Quick bent forward to cut him, he kicked him in the groin. After a grimace and a groan, Quick slapped Buck hard and then held the knife to his throat.

"You hold still. I don't want to kill you just yet, though I will if I have to."

With the knife at Buck's neck, Quick wrapped baling wire around his ankles and knees. When he had secured him, he took another slice with his knife, this one parallel to the first. Buck kept his mouth shut, not giving Quick satisfaction that the knife wounds had hurt him.

"You ain't yelling enough. Maybe you need a little fist first."

Quick began pummeling Buck's face with the flat of his hand, continuing until his eyes had swollen shut and blood trickled from his nose and lips. Despite the beating, Buck refused to moan, cry out, or show any emotion at all. It earned him a kick in the ribs with the toe of Quick's boot.

"I'm going to skin you alive, starting at your neck. If you cry for me, I might be merciful and kill you a little early. Then again, maybe not. Oh, and I haven't forgotten about your balls. They'll be gone long before you die."

Quick began a precise incision along Buck's left shoulder blade, moving slowly. Buck was about to gnaw away the skin on the inside of his mouth, wincing from pain though determined not to give Quick the satisfaction.

All his senses heightened, he heard something moving stealthily behind the lunatic with the knife. It was coming toward them. He knew without seeing that it was the panther. He braced for the attack, figuring death by the big black cat would be a quicker and less painful alternative. He didn't have long to wait.

The panther lunged, landing on Jimmy Quick's shoulders and powering him onto Buck's chest. With its fangs buried in Quick's neck, the big black cat shook his victim like a rag doll. Already dead, Quick's lifeless eyes stared at Buck as the cat dragged him into the thick undergrowth of vegetation encompassing Skeleton Creek. Buck soon fell into a stupor, passing out from a combination of the beating and loss of blood. The panther didn't return for him.

When Buck opened his eyes, he saw Esme kneeling beside him, Beauty by her side.

"I was so worried. Beauty awoke me and demanded I follow her. She led me here. Did Quick do this to you?"

"Get me loose and I'll tell you."

Esme stroked the cut across his shoulder blade and then undid the baling wire around his knees and ankles.

"Why did you remove the amulet? You promised me you wouldn't take it off."

Buck didn't answer. When she rolled him over to release his wrists, she saw the remains of the necklace and the rattlesnake pendant clutched in his hands.

"Quick ripped it off of my neck. It never got far away."

Beauty licked his face as Esme kissed him. "Though I'm glad you are alive, I am tired of the constant doctoring you seem to require."

Buck smiled. "Just once more and I promise, I'll be more careful from now on."

Chapter 35

Buck's wounds had almost healed when he rode Lady to Clayton's ranch, Pard following closely behind. A small party was in progress on Clayton's veranda. Trey and Beth, and Jim and Carol Hagen had joined Clayton and KK for the occasion. Maria smiled and shook her head when Buck requested coffee.

"We were starting to get worried," Clayton said. "Glad you could make it."

Seeing the forlorn expression on the young cowboy's face, Beth asked, "Buck, are you okay?"

"Just a little sad."

Clayton grinned. "What's the matter? You look like you just lost your favorite puppy."

Jim and Carol already knew what the matter was. Esme and Beauty had departed Lykaia, perhaps forever.

"I'm okay. The past few weeks have put me in a funk. I'll be fine. Don't let me spoil the party."

Beth, Carol, and KK couldn't bear Buck's unhappy expression. Descending on him like a mother whose child had just stubbed his toe, they proceeded to console him with kisses and hugs.

"My own mother never gave me that kind of attention," Trey said, shaking his head.

Jim agreed. "Neither did mine."

"Hey, at least you two had mothers," Clayton said, grinning at his little joke.

Buck detached himself from the three doting women and settled into a chair with the group, all of them well beyond their first pitcher of cocktails. When Clayton tried to hand him a margarita, Buck waved it off.

"You really made a mess of the last Navigator I gave you. I think I'm going to have to cut you back to an economy class vehicle," Clayton said with a smile.

"You don't need me anymore. Keep your car."

"You're wrong. I realize now I need a full-time security officer. I can think of no one better for the job than you."

"No offense, Clayton. You know I've never been happy working full time for anyone. You fleshed out my bank account to the point I don't need to. If I were married and had kids to worry about, it might be a different story. Guess that's never going to happen."

Hearing the hurt in his voice, Carol patted his hand. "You are young, and I still expect at least one grandchild before I turn sixty."

"You'll both get what you want," Clayton said. "I have an announcement to make. I'm getting married."

Beth and Carol hugged Clayton, and then KK, as Sheriff Hagen, Buck, and Trey pumped Clayton's hand.

"We are so happy for you two," Beth said.

Clayton glanced at KK, and they both laughed. "Not KK," he said, "Lana."

"You are marrying Lana?" Beth blurted.

Clayton held up a placating palm. "It's really no more than a marriage of convenience which will benefit both Lykaia and O'Meara."

"But what about KK?" Carol asked.

"We are a couple and already have a civil union. We'll never separate. Tell them, KK."

"I'm not the jealous type. Clayton can spend as much time at Lykaia as he wants, as long as he takes me with him."

"And this union has a benefit for you, Buck," Clayton said. "We'll have custody of your child at least half of every year. You can spend as much time with him as you want. When you are comfortable letting him know you are his father, we'll see to it that it happens."

"What about me?" Carol asked.

"You're in, Grandma," Clayton said. "This is a win, win situation."

Maria interrupted their banter with yet another pitcher of margaritas.

"Don't anyone worry about driving home. I have more rooms in this place than a hotel and KK, and I love guests. Drink up!"

The honking of a truck horn outside the veranda suddenly riveted everyone's attention. Satchel and Georgia didn't bother knocking as they joined the party.

"You two come in this house," Clayton said. "Maria, we have more guests."

Both dressed in worn jeans, cowboy boots, and colorful Western shirts, Satchel and Georgia looked happier than Buck could remember seeing either of them. They both sported mile-wide grins.

"What about you two?" Sheriff Hagen asked. "Is there a wedding in your future?"

"We're just having a good time, brother," Satchel said, clutching Georgia even closer.

Georgia continued to smile. "I'm in love with this big galoot, and I have Buck to thank."

Satchel agreed. "We both have Buck to thank."

<hr>

The party continued into the night, Trey and Buck finally ducking outside for a talk. The sky was luminous, filled with stars and the bright light of a full moon. Trey gave Buck a high five.

"We did it, my friend. We busted the biggest cattle-rustling ring this state has ever seen. It earned me a big promotion and Beth, and I are getting married."

"Good for you," Buck said.

"What about you? You don't have another girlfriend yet?"

"It's taking me a while to get over losing Esme."

"Where did she go?"

Buck could only shake his head. "She said she had a journey to take. I don't know why, or to where."

Trey patted Buck's shoulder. "You are young and have more gorgeous women hanging around than anyone I know."

"I'm just so depressed. I never had parents, and now I have lost Esme and Beauty."

"You still have Beth and me and don't forget about Pard and Lady, and Jim and Carol. Tell you the truth I'm having a hard time feeling sorry for you."

Buck nodded. "You're right. Pard is a wonderful dog and Lady the most forgiving female I ever met."

"You're worried about your son, aren't you?"

"I'd be lying if I said I'm not. I know Lana, Clayton, and KK have his best interest at heart. I just don't like the idea of playing second-fiddle as a father."

Trey slapped his shoulder. "He'll be fine. You are, and you never had a dad, much less two."

Unable to contain himself, Buck put his arms around Trey and hugged him. "At least I have a brother."

Trey pushed him away. "Quit dribbling on my shoulder, or I'll have to whack you."

"I guess we did bust the biggest cattle-rustling ring in Oklahoma history," Buck said.

"You bet your sweet ass we did, even if you had to tell one whopper of a lie to accomplish it."

"My butt was puckered for a while, though everything worked out. Still, I don't feel right taking money from Clayton, even though he does have more gold than Midas."

"Have him put you on retainer. Then you can help him whenever he needs it, and you'll have your freedom in the meantime."

"Maybe," Buck said. "I'll have to think about it because I'm getting attached to big Navigator's."

"What else? Are you going to be okay?"

"Pard and I may have to take a trip."

"Where to?"

"A sunny beach, maybe."

"Sounds to me like you need one of Maria's margaritas."

As they sat in silence, clouds began cloaking the Oklahoma landscape. When the full moon emerged, it lighted Clayton's backyard, its appearance accompanied by the mournful howl of a distant animal.

"What the hell was that?" Trey asked.

"Wolf, or maybe a big dog," Buck said.

"I've never heard anything quite like it," Trey said. "Must be some kind of wild and wonderful beast."

When Trey glanced at Buck, he realized a broad grin had replaced his former forlorn expression.

"Sounds like my destiny calling," Buck said. "I think I'm ready now for that margarita."

END

Book Notes

Central Oklahoma is a blackjack covered, rolling expanse of lonely mystery. Too rocky for wheat, the fields bounded by dirt roads and barbwire are the home of horses, cattle, coyotes, and deer. Many creeks dissect the terrain and Skeleton Creek is real.

My inspiration for this novel came to me while exploring an abandoned farmhouse sitting on a lonely hill. Native stone masonry surrounded an old well, the remnants of a wooden water bucket lying on the ground beside it. There were no other buildings on the quarter section of land.

I hiked down the hill, avoiding patches of brush and poison nettle, finally reaching a creek that cut through the property. The wall of dirt and rock dropped almost straight down, a distance of at least twenty feet. When I slid down to the bottom of the slope, it dawned on me that it wouldn't be easy climbing back out.

Brush and blackjacks, so thick that they almost blocked out the sun, grew on both sides of the creek. The creek, deeply incised into red Oklahoma earth, was almost like a tunnel, sending my imagination into overdrive.

What hidden mysteries did the narrow waterway mask? What creatures of the night used the creek as a trail? A thousand untold stories began filling my brain.

I now live close to where *Bones of Skeleton Creek* occurs, and I loved writing the novel featuring Buck Mcdivit, my flawed and horny P.I. with a heart of gold, that loves animals and doesn't have an ounce of quit in his body.

If you liked *Bones of Skeleton Creek,* please check out *Ghost of a Chance* and *Blink of an Eye,* Books 1 and 3 of the Paranormal Cowboy series. If you love mystery, thrills, and suspense with a touch of romance, you might also like my French Quarter Mystery series set in New Orleans. Please tell your friends about *Bones of Skeleton Creek* and consider leaving a review at the place where you purchased the book.

Thanks for being a fan. Without wonderful readers like you, my stories would be little more than morning fog wafting across a forgotten lawn before disappearing forever into the Great Unknown.

About the Author

Born on a sleepy bayou, Louisiana Mystery Writer Eric Wilder grew up listening to tales of ghosts, magic, and voodoo. He is the author of ten novels, four cookbooks, many short stories, and Murder Etouffee, a book that defies classification. His two series feature P.I.s adept in the investigation of the paranormal. He lives in Oklahoma, near historic Route 66 with wife Marilyn, three wonderful dogs, and two great cats.